PRAISE FOR ETGAR KERET

"Keret is a brilliant writer . . . completely unlike any writer I know. He is the voice of the next generation."

—Salman Rushdie

"Keret can do more with six strange and funny paragraphs than most writers can with 600 pages." —Kyle Smith, *People*

"I read [*The Nimrod Flipout*] in bed beside my boyfriend who was reading a much less interesting book and I kept shouting, 'Wow' and 'No way' and 'Oh my god' and my boyfriend would say, 'What? what?' and I'd shake my head and say, 'You wouldn't get it. You just have to read it.' After I finished the book I immediately became more deadpan, more ridiculous and more in touch with my own mortality. My boyfriend was impressed with the new me and I told him, 'It's that book, *The Nimrod Flipout*—it's opened up a whole new world for me.' Now he's reading it, just so we can stay on the same plane of reality together."   —Miranda July, *Salon*

"Stories that are short, strange, funny, deceptively casual in tone and affect, stories that sound like a joke but aren't—Etgar Keret is a writer to be taken seriously."

—Yann Martel, author of *Life of Pi*

"[*The Nimrod Flipout* is] the best work of literature to come out of Israel in the last five thousand years—better than Leviticus and nearly as funny. Each page is a cut and polished gem. Do yourself a favor: walk over to the counter and buy this book now."

—Gary Shteyngart, author of *Super Sad True Love Story*

"Etgar Keret's short stories are fierce, funny, full of energy and insight, and at the same time often deep, tragic, and very moving."—Amos Oz, author of *A Tale of Love and Darkness*

"To call Keret apolitical would be to miss a seminal moment in the history of Jewish literature. Indeed, it would be like pigeonholing Isaac Bashevis Singer—at whose knee Keret seems to have learned the art of magic realism, only to use it with more discipline than his master . . . Keret is a cynic who can't manage to shake off his hopefulness—the most reliable kind of narrator there is. His true ancestor may not be Singer but Woody Allen, who, in his earlier years, summoned the gods of fantasy to help argue his most famous philosophical insights. And Keret is exhibiting *Annie Hall*–era talent here, churning out gem after gem."

—Alana Newhouse, *The Washington Post Book World*

"These stories exude a force and zing that some readers will find life-changing." —Jesse Berrett, *San Francisco Chronicle*

ETGAR KERET
SUDDENLY, A KNOCK ON THE DOOR

Born in Tel Aviv in 1967, Etgar Keret is the author of six bestselling story collections. His writing has been published in *The New Yorker, Harper's Magazine, The New York Times, The Paris Review,* and *Zoetrope,* and has frequently been read on *This American Life. Jellyfish,* his first movie as a director along with his wife, Shira Geffen, won the Caméra d'Or prize for best first feature at Cannes in 2007. *Wristcutters: A Love Story,* a film based on his novella *Kneller's Happy Campers,* premiered at Sundance in 2006. In 2010 he was named a Chevalier of France's Order of Arts and Letters.

ALSO BY ETGAR KERET

SUDDENLY,
A KNOCK ON THE DOOR

SUDDENLY,
A KNOCK ON THE DOOR

ETGAR KERET

TRANSLATED FROM THE HEBREW BY MIRIAM SHLESINGER,

SONDRA SILVERSTON, AND NATHAN ENGLANDER

FARRAR, STRAUS AND GIROUX   NEW YORK

Farrar, Straus and Giroux
18 West 18th Street, New York 10011

Distributed in Canada by D&M Publishers, Inc.
Printed in the United States of America
Originally published in Hebrew in 2010
by Zmora-Bitan as *Pit'om Defikah Ba-Delet*
Published in the United States by Farrar, Straus and Giroux
First American edition, 2012

Some of these translations previously appeared, in slightly different form,
in *The New Yorker*, *Harper's Magazine*, *McSweeney's*, *Zoetrope: All-Story*, *Tin
House*, *n+1*, *One Story*, *BOMB* magazine, *THINQon*, *The Yearbook of
Comparative Literature*, *Electric Literature*, *Conjunctions*,
Gulf Coast, and *Pearl Noir!*.

Library of Congress Cataloging-in-Publication Data
Keret, Etgar, 1967–
    [Pit'om defikah ba-delet. English]
    Suddenly, a knock on the door / Etgar Keret ; translated from the Hebrew
by Miriam Shlesinger, Sondra Silverston, and Nathan Englander. — 1st
American ed.
        p.   cm.
    ISBN 978-0-374-53333-5 (alk. paper)
    1. Keret, Etgar, 1967– —Translations into English.   I. Shlesinger,
Miriam, 1947– II. Silverston, Sondra.   III. Englander, Nathan.   IV. Title.

PJ5054.K375 P5813 2012
892.4'36—dc23

2011046350

Designed by Jonathan D. Lippincott

www.fsgbooks.com

1   3   5   7   9   10   8   6   4   2

TO SHIRA

CONTENTS

SUDDENLY,
A KNOCK ON THE DOOR

SUDDENLY, A KNOCK ON THE DOOR

"Tell me a story," the bearded man sitting on my living-room sofa commands. The situation, I must say, is anything but pleasant. I'm someone who *writes* stories, not someone who tells them. And even *that* isn't something I do on demand. The last time anyone asked me to tell him a story, it was my son. That was a year ago. I told him something about a fairy and a ferret—I don't even remember what exactly—and within two minutes he was fast asleep. But the situation is fundamentally different. Because my son doesn't have a beard, or a pistol. Because my son asked for the story nicely, and this man is simply trying to rob me of it.

I try to explain to the bearded man that if he puts his pistol away it will only work in his favor, in our favor. It's hard to think up a story with the barrel of a loaded pistol pointed at your head. But the guy insists. "In this country," he explains, "if you want something, you have to use force." He just got here from Sweden, and in Sweden it's completely different. Over there, if you want something, you ask politely, and most of the time you get it. But not in the stifling, muggy Middle East. All it takes is one week in this place to figure out how things work—or rather, how things don't work. The Palestinians asked for a state, nicely. Did they get one? The hell they did. So they switched to blowing up kids on buses, and people started listening. The settlers wanted a dialogue. Did anyone pick up on it? No way. So they started getting physical, pouring hot oil on the border patrolmen, and suddenly they had an audience. In this country, might makes right, and it doesn't matter if it's about politics, or economics or a parking space. Brute force is the only language we understand.

Sweden, the place the bearded guy made aliya from, is progressive, and is way up there in quite a few areas. Sweden isn't just ABBA or IKEA or the Nobel Prize. Sweden is a world unto itself, and whatever they have, they got by peaceful means. In Sweden, if he'd gone to the Ace of Base soloist, knocked on her door, and asked her to sing for him, she'd have invited him in and made him a cup of tea. Then she'd have pulled out her acoustic guitar from under the bed and played for him. All this with a smile! But here? I mean, if he hadn't been flashing a pistol I'd have thrown him out right away. Look, I try to reason. "'Look' yourself," the bearded guy grumbles, and cocks his pistol. "It's either a story or a bullet between the eyes." I see my choices are limited. The guy means business. "Two people are sitting in a room," I begin. "Suddenly, there's a knock on the door." The bearded guy stiffens, and for a moment I think maybe the story's getting to him, but it isn't. He's listening to something else. There's a knock on the door. "Open it," he tells me, "and don't try anything. Get rid of whoever it is, and do it fast, or this is going to end badly."

The young man at the door is doing a survey. He has a few questions. Short ones. About the high humidity here in summer, and how it affects my disposition. I tell him I'm not interested but he pushes his way inside anyway.

"Who's that?" he asks me, pointing at the bearded guy. "That's my nephew from Sweden," I lie. "His father died in an avalanche and he's here for the funeral. We're just going over the will. Could you please respect our privacy and leave?" "C'mon, man," the pollster says, and pats me on the shoulder. "It's just a few questions. Give a guy a chance to earn a few bucks. They pay me per respondent." He flops down on the sofa, clutching his binder. The Swede takes a seat next to him. I'm still standing, trying to sound like I mean it. "I'm asking you to leave," I tell him. "Your timing is way off." "Way off, eh?" He opens the plastic binder and pulls out a big revolver. "Why's my timing off? 'Cause I'm darker? 'Cause I'm not good enough? When it comes to Swedes, you've got all the time in the world. But for a Moroccan, for a war veteran who left pieces of his spleen behind in Lebanon, you can't spare a fucking minute." I try to reason with him, to tell him it's not that way at all, that he'd simply caught me at a delicate point in my conversation with the Swede. But the pollster raises his revolver to his lips and signals me to shut up. "*Vamos*," he says. "Stop making excuses. Sit down over there, and out with it." "Out with what?" I ask. The truth is, now I'm pretty uptight. The Swede has a pistol too. Things might get out of hand. East is east and west is west, and all that. Different mentalities. Or else the Swede could lose it, simply because he wants the story all to himself. Solo. "Don't get me started," the pollster warns. "I have a short fuse. Out with the story—and make it quick." "Yeah," the Swede chimes in, and pulls out his piece too. I clear my throat, and start all over again. "Three people are sitting in a room." "And no 'Suddenly, there's a knock on the door,'" the Swede announces. The pollster doesn't quite get it, but plays along with him. "Get going," he says. "And no knocking on the door. Tell us something else. Surprise us."

I stop short, and take a deep breath. Both of them are staring at me. How do I always get myself into these situations? I bet things like this never happen to Amos Oz or David Grossman. Suddenly there's a knock on the door. Their gaze turns menacing. I shrug. It's not about me. There's nothing in my story to connect it to that knock. "Get rid of him," the pollster orders me. "Get rid of him, whoever it is." I open the door just a crack. It's a pizza delivery guy. "Are you Keret?" he asks. "Yes," I say, "but I didn't order a pizza." "It says here Fourteen Zamenhoff Street," he snaps, pointing at the printed delivery slip and pushing his way inside. "So what," I say, "I didn't order a pizza." "Family size," he insists. "Half pineapple, half anchovy. Prepaid. Credit card. Just gimme my tip and I'm outta here." "Are you here for a story too?" the Swede interrogates. "What story?" the pizza guy asks, but it's obvious he's lying. He's not very good at it. "Pull it out," the pollster prods. "C'mon, out with the pistol already." "I don't have a pistol," the pizza guy admits awkwardly, and draws a cleaver out from under his cardboard tray. "But I'll cut him into julienne strips unless he coughs up a good one, on the double."

The three of them are on the sofa—the Swede on the right, then the pizza guy, then the pollster. "I can't do it like this," I tell them. "I can't get a story going with the three of you here and your weapons and all that. Go take a walk around the block, and by the time you get back, I'll have something for you." "The asshole's gonna call the cops," the pollster tells the Swede. "What's he thinking, that we were born yesterday?" "C'mon, give us one and we'll be on our way," the pizza guy begs. "A short one. Don't be so anal. Things are tough, you know. Unemployment, suicide bombings, Iranians. People are hungry for something else. What do you think brought law-abiding guys like us this far? We're desperate, man, desperate."

I clear my throat and start again. "Four people are sitting in a room. It's hot. They're bored. The air conditioner's on the blink. One of them asks for a story. The second one joins in, then the third . . ." "That's not a story," the pollster protests. "That's an eyewitness report. It's exactly what's happening here right now. Exactly what we're trying to run away from. Don't you go and dump reality on us like a garbage truck. Use your imagination, man, create, invent, take it all the way."

I nod and start again. "A man is sitting in a room, all by himself. He's lonely. He's a writer. He wants to write a story. It's been a long time since he wrote his last story, and he misses it. He misses the feeling of creating something out of something. That's right—something out of something. Because something out of nothing is when you make something up out of thin air, in which case it has no value. Anybody can do that. But something out of something means it was really there the whole time, inside you, and you discover it as part of something new, that's never happened before. The man decides to write a story about the situation. Not the political situation and not the social situation either. He decides to write a story about the human situation, the human condition. The human condition the way he's experiencing it right now. But he draws a blank. No story presents itself. Because the human condition the way he's experiencing it right now doesn't seem to be worth a story, and he's just about to give up when suddenly . . ." "I warned you already," the Swede interrupts me.

"No knock on the door." "I've got to," I insist. "Without a knock on the door there's no story." "Let him," the pizza guy says softly. "Give him some slack. You want a knock on the door? Okay, have your knock on the door. Just so long as it brings us a story."

LIELAND

Robbie was seven when he told his first lie. His mother had given him a wrinkled old bill and asked him to go buy her a pack of king-size Kents at the grocery store. Robbie bought an ice-cream cone instead. He took the change and hid the coins under a big white stone in the backyard of their apartment building, and when Mother asked him what had happened he told her that a giant redheaded kid who was missing a front tooth tackled him in the street, slapped him, and took the money. She believed him. And Robbie hasn't stopped lying since. When he was in high school he spent an entire week vegging out on the beach in Eilat, after selling the student counselor a story about his aunt from Beersheba who discovered she had cancer. When he was in the army, this imaginary aunt went blind and saved his ass, big-time, when he went AWOL. No detention, not even confined-to-barracks. Nothing. Once, when he was two hours late for work, he'd made up a lie about a German shepherd he'd found sprawled out beside the road. The dog had been run over, he'd said, and he'd taken it to the vet. In this lie, the dog was paralyzed in two legs, and he'd taken it to the vet only to find that the dog was never going to be able to move his hind legs again.

That did the trick. There were lots of lies along the way in Robbie's life. Lies without arms, lies that were ill, lies that did harm, lies that could kill. Lies on foot, or behind the wheel, black-tie lies, and lies that could steal. He made up these lies in a flash, never thinking he'd have to cross paths with them again.

It all started with a dream. A short, fuzzy dream about his dead mother. In this dream the two of them were sitting on a straw mat in the middle of a clear white surface that seemed to have no beginning and no end. Next to them on this infinite white surface was a gumball machine with a bubble top, the old-fashioned kind where you put a coin in the slot, turn the handle—and out comes a gumball. And in his dream, Robbie's mother told him that the afterworld was driving her up the wall, because the people were good, but there were no cigarettes. Not just no cigarettes, no coffee. No public radio. Nothing.

"You have to help me, Robbie," she said. "You have to buy me a gumball. I raised you, son. All these years I gave you everything and asked for nothing. But now it's time to give something back to your old mom. Buy me a gumball. A red one, if you can, but blue is okay too." And in his dream, Robbie kept rummaging through his pockets, hoping to find some change. Nothing. "I don't have any, Mom," he said, the tears welling up in his eyes. "I don't have any change. I went through all my pockets."

Considering that he never cried when he was awake, it was strange to be crying in his dream. "Did you look under the stone?" his mother asked, and clasped his hand in her own. "Maybe the coins are still there?"

And then he woke up. It was five a.m. on a Saturday, and

still dark outside. Robbie found himself getting into the car and driving to the place where he had lived as a little boy. With no traffic on the road, it took him less than twenty minutes to get there. On the ground floor of the building, where Pliskin's grocery store had once been, there was a dollar store, and next to it, instead of the shoe-repair guy there was a cellphone outlet offering upgrades like there was no tomorrow.

But the building itself hadn't changed. More than twenty years had gone by since they'd moved out, and it hadn't even been repainted. The yard was still the same too, a few flowers, a spigot, a rusty water meter, weeds. And in the corner, next to the clotheslines, was the white stone, just lying there.

He stood in the backyard of the building where he'd grown up, wearing his parka, holding a big plastic flashlight, feeling strange. Five thirty a.m. on a Saturday. Let's say a neighbor showed up—what would he say? My dead mother appeared in my dream and asked me to buy her a gumball, so I came here to look for change?

Strange that the stone was still there, after all those years. Then again, if you thought about it, it's not as if stones just get up and walk away. He picked it up, gingerly, as if there might be a scorpion hiding beneath it. But there was no scorpion, and no snake either, and no coins. Just a hole the width of a grapefruit, and a light shining out of it.

Robbie tried to peek into the hole, but the light dazzled him. He hesitated for a second, then reached in. Lying on the ground, he extended his arm all the way up to his shoulder, trying to touch something at the bottom. But there was no bottom and the only thing he could reach was made of cold metal and felt like a handle. The handle of a gumball machine. Robbie turned it as hard as he could and felt the handle respond to his touch. This was the moment the gumball should have rolled out. This was exactly when it should have made its way from the metallic innards of the machine into the hand of the little boy waiting impatiently for it to emerge. This was exactly the moment when all those things were supposed to happen. But they didn't. And as soon as Robbie had finished turning the handle, he'd showed up here.

"Here" was a different place, but a familiar one too. It was the place from his mother's dream. Stark white, no walls, no floor, no ceiling, no sunshine. Just whiteness and a gumball machine. A gumball machine and a sweaty, ugly redheaded boy. Somehow, Robbie hadn't noticed him before, and just as Robbie was about to smile at the boy or say anything at all, the redhead kicked him in the shins, as hard as he could, and Robbie dropped to the ground, writhing in pain. With Robbie down on his knees, he and the kid were now the same height. The kid looked Robbie in the eye, and even though Robbie knew they'd never met, there was something familiar about him. "Who are you?" he asked the kid, who was standing in front of him. "Me?" the kid answered, showing a mean smile with a missing front tooth. "I'm your first lie."

Robbie struggled to his feet. His leg hurt like hell. The kid himself was long gone. Robbie studied the gumball machine. In among the round gumballs there were half-transparent plastic balls with trinkets inside them. He rummaged through his pockets for some change, but then remembered that the kid had grabbed his wallet before he took off.

Robbie limped away, in no particular direction. Since there was nothing to go by on the white surface, except the gumball machine, all he could do was try to move away from it. Every few steps he turned around to make sure the machine was becoming smaller.

At one point, he turned around to discover a German shepherd standing next to a skinny old man with a glass eye and no arms. The dog he recognized at once, by the way it half-crawled forward, its two forelegs struggling to pull its paralyzed pelvis along. It was the run-over dog from the lie. It was panting with the effort and excitement, and was happy to see him. It licked Robbie's hand and looked at him intently with glistening eyes. Robbie couldn't quite place the skinny old man.

"I'm Robbie," he said.

"I'm Igor," the old man introduced himself, and gave Robbie a pat with one of his hooks.

"Do we know each other?" Robbie asked after a few seconds' awkward silence.

"No," Igor said, lifting the leash with one of his hooks. "I'm only here because of him. He sniffed you from miles away and got worked up. He wanted us to come."

"So, there's no connection—between us?" Robbie asked. He felt a sense of relief as he said this.

"Me and you? No, no connection whatsoever. I'm somebody else's lie."

Robbie almost asked whose lie he was but he was afraid the question might be considered rude in this place. For that matter, he'd have liked to ask what this place was exactly and whether there were a lot more people there, or more lies, or whatever they called themselves, other than him. But he thought it might be a sensitive topic and that he shouldn't bring it up just yet. So instead of talking, he patted Igor's handicapped dog. It was a nice dog, and it seemed happy to meet Robbie, who wished his lie had had a little less pain and suffering in it.

"The gumball machine," he asked Igor, when a few minutes had passed. "What coins does it take?"

"Liras," the old man said.

Robbie said, "There was a kid here just now. He took my wallet. But even if he hadn't, there wouldn't be any liras in it."

"A kid with a tooth missing?" Igor asked. "That little scum steals from everyone. He even eats the dog's Ken-L Ration. Where I come from, in Russia, they'd take a kid like that and stick him out in the snow in nothing but his underwear, and they wouldn't let him back in the house until his whole body turned blue." With one of his hooks, Igor pointed to his back pocket. "In there I've got some liras. Help yourself. It's on me."

Robbie hesitated, but he took a lira coin out of Igor's pocket and, after thanking him, offered to give him his Swatch in return.

"Thanks." Igor nodded. "But what would I do with a plastic watch? Besides, I'm in no hurry to get anywhere."

When he saw Robbie looking around for something else to give him, Igor stopped him and said, "I owe you anyway. If you hadn't made up that lie about the dog, I'd be all alone. So now we're even."

Robbie hobbled back as quickly as he could in the direction of the gumball machine. He was still smarting from the redhead's kick, but less so now. He dropped the lira into the slot, took a deep breath, closed his eyes, and turned the handle.

He found himself stretched out on the ground in the yard of their old building. The dawn light was painting the sky dark shades of blue. Robbie pulled his arm out of the hole in the ground. And when he opened his fist, there was a red gumball inside.

Before he left, he put the stone back in its place. He didn't ask himself about the hole and what exactly had happened down there. He just got in the car, backed up, and drove away. The red gumball he put under his pillow, for his mother, in case she came back in his dream.

At first, Robbie thought about it a lot, about that place, about the dog, about Igor, about other lies he'd told—lies he was lucky enough not to have to meet again. There was that bizarre lie he'd told his ex-girlfriend, Ruthie, when he couldn't make it to Friday-night dinner at her parents' house—about this niece of his who lived in Natanya whose husband beat her up, and about how the guy had threatened to kill her, so Robbie had to go over there to help calm things down. To this day, he had no idea why he'd made up such a twisted story. Maybe at the time he thought that the more complicated and warped it was, the more likely Ruthie was to believe him. Some people when they bail on Friday-night dinner say they've got a headache or something. Not him. Instead, because of him and those stories of his, a lunatic husband and a battered wife were out there, not far away, in a hole in the ground.

He didn't go back to the hole, but something about that place stuck with him. At first, he continued to tell lies, but they were the kind where nobody beats anybody and nobody limps or dies of cancer. For example: He was late for work because he had to water the plants in his aunt's apartment while she was visiting her successful son in Japan. Or: He was late for a baby shower because a cat just had kittens on his stoop and he had to take care of the litter. Stuff like that.

But it was much harder to make up all the positive lies. At least, if you wanted them to sound plausible. In general if you tell people something bad, they buy right into it, because it strikes them as normal. But when you make up good things, they get suspicious. And so, very gradually, Robbie found himself winding down the lies. Out of laziness, mostly. And with time, he thought less and less about that place. About the hole. Until the morning when he overheard Natasha from Accounting talking to her boss. Her uncle Igor had had a heart attack and she needed some time off. Poor guy—a widower, who'd already lost both arms in an accident in Russia. And now, his heart. He was so alone, so helpless.

The head of Accounting granted her time off right away, no questions asked. She went to her office, took her bag, and left the building. Robbie followed Natasha to her car. When she stopped to get her keys out of her bag, he stopped too. She turned around. "You work in Acquisitions, don't you?" she asked. "Aren't you Zaguri's assistant?"

"Yeah," Robbie said, nodding. "My name's Robbie."

"Cool, Robbie," Natasha said with a nervous Russian smile. "So what's up? You need something?"

"It's about that lie you told, earlier, to the head of Accounting," Robbie stammered. "I know him."

"You followed me all the way to my car just to accuse me of being a liar?"

"No," said Robbie. "I didn't mean to accuse you. Really. Your being a liar is cool. I'm a liar too. But this Igor from your lie, I met him. He's one in a million. And you—if you don't mind my saying so—you've made things pretty hard for him as it is. So I just wanted to—"

"Would you get out of my way?" Natasha interrupted him icily. "You're blocking the door of my car."

"I know this sounds far-fetched, but I can prove it," Robbie said, feeling more and more uneasy. "This Igor doesn't have an eye. I mean, he does, but only one. At one point, you must have made up something about how he'd lost an eye, right?"

Natasha was already getting into her car, but she stopped. "Where d'you get that from? Are you a friend of Slava's?"

"I don't know any Slava," Robbie muttered. "Just Igor. Really. If you want, I can take you to him."

They were standing in the backyard of his building. Robbie moved the stone aside, lay down on the damp soil, and pushed his arm all the way into the hole. Natasha was standing over him. He held out his other arm and said, "Hold on tight."

Natasha looked at the man stretched out at her feet. Thirty-something, good-looking, in a clean, ironed white shirt, which was already slightly less clean and much less ironed. His one arm was stuck in the hole, his cheek was glued to the ground.

"Hold tight," he said. And as she held out her hand to him, she couldn't help wondering how it was she always wound up with the oddballs. When he'd started with that crap by the car, she thought maybe it was a cute way of hitting on her, but now she realized that this guy with the soft eyes and the bashful smile really was a nutcase. His fingers were clasping hers. They stayed that way, frozen, for a minute or so, him on the ground, and her standing over him, slightly stooped, looking bewildered.

"Okay," Natasha whispered in a gentle, almost therapeutic voice. "So we're holding hands. Now what?"

"Now," Robbie said, "I'll turn the handle."

It took them a long time to find Igor. First they met a hairy, hunchbacked lie, evidently Argentinian, who spoke nothing but Spanish. Then, another of Natasha's lies—an overzealous policeman with a yarmulke, who insisted on detaining them and checking their papers, but he'd never even heard of Igor. In the end the person who helped them out was Robbie's battered niece from Natanya. They found her feeding the litter from his most recent lie. She hadn't seen Igor for a few days, but she knew where to find his dog. As for the dog, once it finished licking Robbie's hands and face, it was glad to take them to Igor's bedside.

Igor was in pretty bad shape. His complexion was sallow and he was sweating heavily. But when he saw Natasha, his face lit up. He was so thrilled that he hauled himself up and hugged her, even though he could hardly stand. At that point, Natasha began to cry and asked him to forgive her because this Igor wasn't just one of her lies, he was also her uncle. A made-up uncle, but still. And Igor told her she shouldn't feel bad, the life she invented for him may not always have been easy, but he'd enjoyed every minute of it, and she had nothing to worry about, because compared to the train crash in Minsk, the stickup in Odessa, the lightning that struck him in Vladivostok, and the pack of rabid wolves in Siberia, this heart attack was small change. And when they got back to the gumball machine, Robbie put in a one-lira coin, took Natasha's hand, and asked her to turn the handle.

Once they were back in the yard, Natasha found herself holding a plastic ball, with a trinket inside: an ugly, gold-colored charm in the shape of a heart.

"You know," she said, "I was supposed to be going to Sinai tonight with a friend, for a few days, but I think I'm going to call it off, and go back tomorrow to take care of Igor. Would you like to come too?"

Robbie nodded. He knew that if he wanted to join her, he'd have to come up with another lie at the office. He wasn't quite sure what it would be. All he knew was that it would be a happy lie, full of light, flowers, and sunshine. And who knows—maybe even a baby or two, and they'd be smiling.

CHEESUS CHRIST

Have you ever wondered what word is most frequently uttered by people about to die a violent death? MIT carried out a comprehensive study of the question among heterogeneous communities in North America and discovered that the word is none other than *fuck*. Eight percent of those about to die say "What the fuck," 6 percent say only "Fuck," and there's another 2.8 percent that say "Fuck you," though in their case, of course, *you* is the last word, even if *fuck* overshadows it irrefutably. And what does Jeremy Kleinman say a minute before he checks out? He says, "Without cheese." Jeremy says that because he's ordering something in a cheeseburger restaurant called Cheesus Christ. They don't have plain hamburgers on the menu, so Jeremy, who keeps kosher, asks for a cheeseburger without cheese. The shift manager in the restaurant doesn't make a big deal out of it. Lots of customers have asked her for that in the past, so many that she felt the need to report on it in a series of detailed e-mails to the CEO of the Cheesus Christ chain, whose office is in Atlanta. She suggested that he add a plain hamburger to the menu. "A lot of people ask me for it, but at the moment, they have to order a cheeseburger without cheese, which is cagey and a little embarrassing. It's embarrassing for me, and, if you don't mind my saying so, for the whole chain. It makes me feel like a technocrat, and for the customers, the chain comes off as an inflexible organization they have to trick in order to get what they want." The CEO never replied to her e-mails, and for her, that was even more embarrassing and humiliating than all those times customers asked her for cheeseburgers without cheese. When a dedicated employee turns to her employer with a problem, especially one related to the workplace, the least he can do is acknowledge her existence. The CEO could have written her that it was being handled or that, while he appreciated her turning to him, he unfortunately couldn't make any changes to the menu, or a million other bullshit replies of that kind. But he didn't. He didn't write anything. And that made her feel like she was invisible. Just like that night in New Haven when her boyfriend Nick started hitting on the waitress while she herself was sitting next to him at the bar. She'd cried then, and Nick hadn't even known why, and that same night, she'd packed her things and left. Mutual friends had called a few weeks later to tell her Nick had killed himself. None of them openly blamed her for what happened, but there was something in the way they told her about it, something accusing, though she couldn't even say what. In any case, when the CEO didn't answer her e-mails, she thought about quitting her job. But what happened with Nick stopped her from doing that, and it wasn't as if she thought the CEO of Cheesus Christ would commit suicide when he heard that the shift manager of some crummy branch in the Northeast had quit, but still. The truth is that if the CEO had heard she'd quit because of him, he actually would have killed himself. The truth is that if the CEO had heard that the African white lion had become extinct because of illegal hunting, he would have killed himself. He would even have killed himself after hearing something more trivial, for instance, that it was going to rain tomorrow. The CEO of the Cheesus Christ restaurant chain suffered from severe clinical depression. His colleagues at work knew that, but were careful not to spread this painful fact around, mostly because they respected his privacy, but also because it could have instantly sent stock prices crashing. After all, what does the stock market sell us if not the unfounded hope of a rosy future? And a CEO with clinical depression is not exactly the ideal ambassador for that kind of message. The CEO of Cheesus Christ, who totally understood how problematic his emotional state was, both personally and publicly, tried medication. That didn't help at all. The pills were prescribed to him by a doctor from Iraq who had been granted refugee status in the United States after his family was accidentally blown up by an F-16 trying to assassinate Saddam Hussein's sons. His wife, father, and two small sons were killed, and only his older daughter, Suha, survived. In an interview on CNN, the doctor said that despite his personal tragedy, he wasn't angry at the American people. But the truth is that he was. He was more than angry. He was boiling with rage toward the American people. But he knew that if he wanted a green card, he had to lie about it. As he lied, he thought about his dead family and his living daughter. He lied because he believed that an American education would be good for her. How wrong he was. His daughter became pregnant at fifteen by some fat white-trash kid who was a year ahead of her at school and refused to acknowledge the baby. Due to complications at birth, the baby was born retarded. In the States, just like almost anywhere else, when you're a fifteen-year-old single mother of a retarded child, for all intents and purposes, your fate is sealed. There's probably some made-for-TV movie that claims that isn't the case, that you can still find love and have a career and who knows what else. But that's only a movie. In real life, the minute they told her that her baby was retarded it was as if a GAME OVER sign in neon lights was flashing in the air above her head. Maybe if her father had told the truth on CNN and they hadn't gone to the States, her fate would have been different. And if Nick hadn't hit on that bottle blonde in the bar, his situation and the shift manager's would have been much better too. And if the CEO of the Cheesus Christ chain had gotten the right medication, his situation would have been just great. And if that crazy guy in the cheeseburger restaurant hadn't stabbed Jeremy Kleinman, Jeremy Kleinman's state would be alive, which in most people's opinion is a lot better than the dead state he now found himself in. He didn't die right away. He gasped, tried to say something, but the shift manager, who was holding his hand, told him not to speak, to save his strength. He didn't speak, he tried to save his strength. Tried, but couldn't. There's a theory, also out of MIT, I think, about the butterfly effect: a butterfly flutters its wings on a beach in Brazil, and as a result, a tornado starts up on the other side of the world. The tornado appears in the original example. They could have thought up a different example in which the flutter of butterfly wings causes badly needed rain, but the scientists who developed the theory chose a tornado, and not because, like the CEO of Cheesus Christ, they were clinically depressed. It's because the scientists who specialize in probability know that the chance of something detrimental occurring is a thousand times greater than the chance of something beneficial happening. "Hold my hand" is what Jeremy Kleinman wanted to say to the shift manager as his life leaked out of him like chocolate milk from a punctured carton. "Hold it and don't let go, whatever happens." But he didn't say that because she asked him not to speak. He didn't say that because he didn't need to—she held his sweaty hand till he died. For a long time after that, actually. She held his hand till the paramedics asked her if she was his wife. Three days later, she got an e-mail from the CEO. That incident in her branch had made him decide to sell the chain and retire. The decision brought him far enough out of his depression to make him start answering his e-mails. He answered them from his laptop, sitting on a gorgeous beach in Brazil. In his long e-mail, he wrote that she was absolutely right and he would pass on her carefully reasoned request to the new CEO. As he pressed SEND, his finger touched the wings of a butterfly sleeping on the keyboard. The butterfly fluttered its wings. Somewhere on the other side of the world, evil winds began to blow.

SIMYON

Two people were standing at the door. A second lieutenant wearing a knitted yarmulke, and behind him, a thin officer with sparse, light-colored hair and captain's bars on her shoulders. Orit waited a minute, and when she saw that they still weren't saying anything, she asked if she could help them. "Druckman," the captain tossed the word, part command, part reprimand, at the soldier. "It's about your husband," the religious soldier mumbled at Orit. "Can we come in?" Orit smiled and said that this must be some kind of mistake because she wasn't married. The captain looked down at the wrinkled note she was holding and asked if her name was Orit, and when Orit said yes, the captain said politely but firmly, "Could we come in for a minute anyway?" Orit led them into the living room of the apartment she shared with her roommate. Before she had a chance to offer them something to drink, the religious soldier blurted out, "He's dead." "Who?" Orit asked. "Why now?" the captain rebuked him. "Can't you wait a second for her to sit down? To get herself a glass of water?" "I apologize," the religious soldier said to Orit, clenching his lips in a nervous twitch. "This is my first. I'm still training." "It's all right," Orit said, "but who's dead?" "Your husband," the religious soldier said. "I don't know whether you heard, but this morning there was a terrorist attack at the Beit Leed junction . . ." "No," Orit said, "I haven't heard. I don't listen to the news. But it doesn't matter anyway because this is a mistake. I told you, I'm not married." The religious soldier gave the captain a pleading look. "You're Orit Bielsky?" the captain asked in a slightly impatient voice. "No," Orit said, "I'm Orit Levine." "Right," the captain replied. "Right. And in February two years ago, you married First Sergeant Simyon Bielsky." Orit sat down on the torn living-room couch. The inside of her throat was so dry that it itched. On second thought, it really would've been better if that Druckman had waited till she got herself a glass of Diet Coke before starting. "So I don't get it," the religious soldier whispered out loud, "is it her or isn't it?" The captain signaled him to shut up. She went over to the kitchen sink and brought back a glass of water for Orit. The water from the faucet in the apartment was disgusting. Orit always thought water was disgusting, especially the water in the apartment. "Take your time," the captain said, handing Orit the glass. "We're in no rush," she said, and sat down beside her. They sat like that, in absolute silence, until the religious soldier, who was still standing, started to lose his patience and said, "He didn't have any family here, you probably know that?" Orit nodded. "They all stayed in Russia or the CIS, or whatever they call it now. He was completely alone." "Except for you," the captain said, touching Orit's hand with her own dry one. "Do you know what that means?" Druckman asked, sitting down on an armchair across from them. "Shut up," the captain hissed at him. "You idiot." "Why an idiot?" the religious soldier asked, insulted. "We'll have to tell her in the end anyway, so why drag it out?" The captain ignored him and gave Orit an awkward hug that seemed to embarrass them both. "Have to tell me what?" Orit asked, trying to extricate herself from the hug. The captain let go, took a slightly theatrical deep breath, and said, "You're the only one who can identify him."

She'd met Simyon for the first time on the day they got married. He was serving on the same base as Assi, and Assi always used to tell her stories about him, how he wore his pants so high that every morning he had to decide which side to put his prick on, and how every time they listened to the regards-to-soldiers radio program, when the announcer said something like "To the cutest soldier in the army," Simyon would always tense up, as if the message was 100 percent for him. "Who could be sending regards to that shmuck?" Assi would say, laughing. And that's the shmuck she married. The truth was that she'd suggested to Assi that he should be the one to marry her so she wouldn't have to serve in the army, but Assi said no way, because a fictitious marriage to a boyfriend was never completely fictitious, and it was a sure way to mess things up. He was also the one who suggested Simyon. "For a hundred shekels, that moron would even make you a baby," Assi said with a laugh. "For a hundred shekels, those Russians would do anything." She told Assi that she had to think about it, even though in her heart she'd already agreed. But he'd hurt her feelings when he said he wouldn't marry her. She was just asking him for a favor, and a boyfriend should know how to help when he's needed. Besides, even if it was only fictitious, it was no fun being married to a shmuck.

The next day, Assi came home from the base, planted a wet kiss on her forehead, and said, "I saved you a hundred shekels." Orit wiped the saliva off her forehead and Assi explained: "That moron will marry you for free." Orit said that seemed a little suspicious and they had to be careful, because maybe that Simyon didn't really understand what the word *fictitious* meant. "Oh, he understands all right," Assi said, and started foraging around in the refrigerator. "He may be a complete idiot, but he's cagey like you wouldn't believe." "So why did he agree to do it for free?" Orit asked. "How do I know?" Assi said, laughing and taking a bite of an unwashed cucumber. "Maybe he figured out that it was as close to being married as he'd ever get in this life."

The captain drove the Renault and the religious soldier sat in the back. They were quiet almost all the way, and that left Orit a lot of time to think about the fact that she was going to see a dead person for the first time in her life, and that she always found herself bastards for boyfriends and that even though she knew it from the first minute, she still always stayed with them for a year or two. She thought about the abortion and about her mother, who believed in reincarnation and insisted afterward that the baby's soul was reincarnated in her scrawny cat. "Listen to the way he's crying," she told Orit. "Listen to his voice, it's like a baby's. You've had him for four years already and he never cried like that." Orit knew that her mother was talking crap and that the cat was just sniffing food or some female cat out the window. Except that his yowling really did sound a little like a baby crying and he went at it all night. Her only piece of luck was that she and Assi weren't together anymore, because if she'd told him something like that, he would have burst out laughing. She tried to think about Simyon's soul too, and where it had been reincarnated, but she reminded herself that she didn't believe in any of that. Then she asked herself why she'd agreed to go to the morgue with the officers, and why she hadn't mentioned that the marriage was fictitious. There was something weird about going to a morgue and identifying a husband. Scary, but exciting too. It was a little like being in a movie—having the experience without paying the price. Assi would probably say that it was a terrific opportunity to get a lifetime widow's pension from the army without even lifting a finger, and no one in the army could do anything against a marriage contract from the Rabbinate. "It'll be fine," said the captain, who must have noticed the thought lines in Orit's forehead. "We'll be with you the whole time."

Assi came to the Rabbinate as Simyon's witness, and throughout the ceremony he made faces, trying to get Orit to laugh. Simyon himself looked a lot better than the stories about him made out. Not a world-class hunk, but not as ugly as Assi'd described him. And he wasn't such an idiot either. He was very strange, but not stupid, and after the Rabbinate, Assi took them out for falafel. That whole day, Simyon and Orit didn't exchange a word except for *hello* and the words they had to speak at the ceremony, and later at the falafel stand, they tried hard not to look at each other. That made Assi laugh. "Look at how pretty your wife is," he said, putting his hand on Simyon's shoulder. Simyon kept his eyes fixed on the dripping pita bread he was holding. "What are we going to do with you, Simyon?" Assi said, still needling him. "You know that now you have to kiss her. Otherwise, according to Jewish law, the marriage isn't valid." To this day, she doesn't really know whether Simyon believed him. Assi told her later that of course he hadn't, and that he was just taking advantage of the situation, but Orit wasn't so sure. In any case, he suddenly bent forward and tried to kiss her. Orit jumped back, and his lips didn't touch hers. But the smell from his mouth did, blending with the smell of frying falafel oil and that moldy smell of the Rabbinate that clung to her hair. She took a few steps away from them and vomited into a flower box, and when she looked up, her eyes met Simyon's. He froze for a minute and then started to run, to get away. Assi tried to call him back, but he didn't stop. And that was the last time she saw him. Till today.

On the way to the morgue, she was afraid she wouldn't be able to identify him. After all, she'd seen him only once, two years ago, and he was alive and well then. But now she knew right away that it was him. A green sheet covered his body up to his neck. His face was completely intact, except for a small hole no larger that a one-shekel coin in his cheek. And the smell of the corpse was just like the smell of his breath on her face two years ago. She'd thought about that moment many times. While they were still at the falafel stand, Assi had told her that it wasn't her fault that Simyon had bad breath, but she always felt like it was. And today, when they knocked on the door, she should have remembered him. It wasn't as if she'd gotten married a million times or anything. "Do you want us to give you a minute alone with your husband?" the captain asked. Orit shook her head. "Really. It's okay to cry," the captain said. "There's no point in holding it in."

SHUT

I know a guy who fantasizes all the time. I mean, this guy even walks down the street with his eyes shut. One day, I'm sitting in the passenger seat of his car and I look over to the left and see him with both his hands on the wheel and his eyes shut. No kidding, he was driving like that on a main street.

"Haggai," I say, "that's not a good idea. Haggai, open your eyes." But he keeps driving like everything's fine.

"You know where I am now?" he asks me.

"Open your eyes," I say again, "come on, it's freaking me out." Miraculously, we didn't crash.

The guy would fantasize about other people's homes, that they were his. About their cars, about their jobs. Never mind their jobs. About his wife. He'd imagine that other women were his wife. And kids, too, kids he met in the street or the park, or saw on some TV series, imagining they were his family instead of his own kids. He'd spend hours doing it. If it was up to him, he'd spend his whole life at it.

"Haggai," I say to him, "Haggai, wake up. Wake up to your own life. You have an amazing life. A fantastic wife. Great kids. Wake up."

"Stop," he answers from the depths of his beanbag, "don't

ruin it. You know who I'm with now? Yotam Ratsabi, my old army buddy. I'm on a jeep tour with Yotam Ratsabi. Just me, Yoti, and little Eviatar Mendelssohn. He's this wiseass kid from Amit's kindergarten. And Eviatar, the little devil, says to me, 'Dad, I'm thirsty. Can I have a beer?' Picture it. The kid's not seven yet. So I say, 'No beer, Evi. You know Mom says it's not allowed.' His mom, my ex, I mean. Rona Yedidia from high school. Beautiful as a model, but tough, tough as nails."

"Haggai," I say, "he's not your kid and she's not your wife. You're not divorced, man, you're happily married. Open your eyes."

"Every time I bring the kid home to her, I get a hard-on," he says, like he doesn't hear me. "A hard-on as big as a ship's mast. She's beautiful, my ex, beautiful but tough. And that toughness is what gives me a hard-on."

"She's not your ex," I say, "and you don't have a hard-on." I know what I'm talking about. He's a meter away from me in his shorts. No hard-on there.

"We had to split," he says, "I hated being with her. And she hated being with herself too."

"Haggai," I plead, "your wife's name is Carnie. And yes, she's beautiful. But she's not tough. Not with you." His wife is really soft. She has the gentle soul of a bird and a big heart; she feels for everybody. We've been together for nine months now. Haggai starts work early, so I go to see her at eight thirty, right after she drops the kids off at kindergarten.

"Rona and I met in high school," he goes on. "She was my first and I was hers. After the divorce, I fucked around a lot, but none of the women even came close to her. And, you know, at least from a distance, she looks like she's still alone. If I found out she has someone, it would shatter me, even though we're divorced and all. Shatter me into pieces. I just wouldn't be able to take it. None of the other women mean anything. Just her. She's the one who's always been there."

"Haggai," I say, "her name's Carnie and no one's with her. You're still married."

"No one's with Rona either," he says, and licks his dry lips, "no one. I'd kill myself if there was."

Carnie comes into the apartment now, carrying an AM/PM bag. She tosses a casual "Hi" in my direction. Since we've been together, she tries to be more distant when other people are around. She doesn't even say hi to Haggai; she knows there's no point talking to him when his eyes are shut.

"My house," he says, "right in the center of Tel Aviv. Beautiful, with a mulberry tree right outside the window. But it's small, way too small. I need another room. On the weekends, when I have the kids, I have to open the living-room couch. It's a real pain in the neck. If I don't find a solution by summer, I'll just have to move."

HEALTHY START

Every night, ever since she'd left him, he'd fall asleep in a different spot: on the sofa, in an armchair in the living room, on the mat on the balcony like some homeless bum. And every morning, he made a point of going out for breakfast. Even prisoners get a daily walk in the yard, don't they? At the café they always gave him a table set for two, and sat him across from an empty chair. Always. Even when the waiter specifically asked if he was alone. Other people would sit there in twos or threes, laughing, tasting each other's food, fighting over the check, while Miron sat by himself eating his Healthy Start—orange juice, muesli with honey, decaf double espresso with warm low-fat milk on the side. Of course it would have been nicer if someone had been sitting across the table from him and laughing with him, if there had been someone to argue with over the check as he struggled to pay, handing over the money to the waitress, saying, "Don't take it from him! Avri, put it back. This one's on me." But he didn't really have anyone to do that with, and breakfast alone in a café was a hundred times better than staying at home.

Miron spent a lot of time eyeing the other tables. He'd eavesdrop on conversations, read the sports supplement, or examine the ups and downs of the Israeli shares on Wall Street with an air of detached concern. Sometimes someone would come over and ask for a section of the paper he'd finished reading, and he would nod and try to smile. Once, when a sexy young mother with a baby in a stroller walked over to him, he even said to her, as he gave up the front page with the banner headline about a gang rape in the suburbs: "What a crazy world we're bringing our children into." He thought it sounded like the kind of statement that brings people closer together, pointing as it did to their common fate, but the sexy mom just glared at him and took the Healthy Living supplement, too, without asking.

Then one Thursday a fat, sweaty guy walked into the café and smiled at him. Miron was caught off guard. The last person to give him a smile was Maayan, just before she left him, five months earlier, and her smile had been unmistakably sarcastic, whereas this one was soft, almost apologetic. The fat guy gestured something, apparently a signal that he'd like to sit down, and Miron nodded almost without thinking. The fat guy took a seat.

"Reuben," he said. "Listen, I'm really sorry I'm late. I know we said ten but I had a nightmare morning with the kid."

It crossed Miron's mind that maybe he ought to tell the fat guy he wasn't Reuben, but he found himself checking his watch instead, and saying, "What's ten minutes? Forget it."

Then neither of them spoke for a second, and Miron asked if the kid was okay. And the fat guy said she was, it was just that she'd started a new kindergarten, and every time he took her there she had a hard time letting him go.

"But never mind," he stopped short. "You've got enough on your plate without my problems. Let's get down to business."

Miron took a deep breath and waited.

"Look," the fat guy said. "Five hundred is too high. Give it to me for four hundred. You know what? Four hundred and ten even and I'm good for six hundred pieces."

"Four hundred and eighty," Miron said. "Four hundred and eighty. And that's only if you're good for a thousand."

"You gotta understand," the fat guy said. "The market's in the shitter, what with the recession and all. Just last night on the news they showed people eating out of garbage cans. If you keep pushing, I'll have to sell high. You're pricing me right out of the market."

"Don't worry," Miron told him. "For every three people eating out of garbage cans, there's someone driving a Mercedes."

This made the fat guy laugh out loud. "They told me you were tough," he muttered with a smile.

"I'm just like you," Miron protested. "Simply trying to keep body and soul together."

The fat guy wiped his sweaty palm on his shirt, then held it out. "Four hundred and sixty," he said. "Four hundred and sixty and I take a thousand." When he saw Miron wasn't reacting, he added: "Four hundred and sixty, a thousand pieces, and I owe you a favor. And you know better than anyone, Reuben, that in our business favors are worth more than money."

This last sentence was all Miron needed to take the outstretched hand and shake it. For the first time in his life, someone owed him a favor. Someone who thought his name was Reuben, but still. And when they'd finished eating, as they argued over who would pick up the tab, a warm feeling spread through Miron's stomach. He beat the fat guy to it by a tenth of a second and shoved the crumpled bill into the waitress's hand.

From that day on it became practically standard procedure. Miron would take a seat, give his order, and keep a look-out for any new person who walked into the café, and if that person started searching the tables with an expectant look, Miron would quickly wave and invite him or her to join him.

"I don't want this to end up in court," a bald guy with thick eyebrows told him.

"Me neither," Miron conceded. "It's always better to settle things amicably."

"Just remember I don't do night shifts," a Botox-lipped bleach blonde announced.

"Just what do you expect? Everyone else will do night shifts except you?" Miron grumbled back.

"Gabi asked me to tell you he's sorry," said a guy with rotting teeth and an earring.

"If he really was sorry," Miron countered, "he should have come and told me himself. No middlemen!"

"In your e-mail you sounded taller," a skinny redhead complained. "In your e-mail you sounded less picky," Miron snapped.

And somehow everything worked out in the end. He and Baldy settled out of court. Botox Lips agreed to ask her sister to babysit so she could do one night shift a week. Rotting Teeth promised Gabi would phone, and the redhead and Miron agreed they weren't quite right for each other. Sometimes they picked up the tab, sometimes he did. With the redhead, they split the bill. And it was all so fascinating, that if a whole morning went by when nobody took a seat across from him at the table, Miron felt let down. Luckily, this didn't happen too often.

Almost two months had passed since the meeting with

the sweaty fat guy when a man with a pockmarked face walked in. Despite his skin and the fact that he looked at least ten years older than Miron, he was good-looking with loads of charisma. The first thing he said as he sat down was: "I was sure you wouldn't show."

"But we agreed to meet," Miron answered.

"Yes," said the pockmarked guy with a sad smile, "except that after the way I yelled at you on the phone, I was afraid you'd chicken out."

"So here I am," Miron said, almost teasingly.

"I'm sorry I yelled at you on the phone," the guy apologized. "Really, I just lost it. But I meant every word I said—you got that? I'm asking you to stop seeing her."

"But I love her," Miron said in a choked voice.

"Sometimes you can love something and you still have to give it up," the pockmarked guy said. "Listen to someone a little older than you. Sometimes you have to give it up."

"Sorry," Miron said, "but I can't."

"Yes you can," the guy shot back. "You can and you will. There's no other way. Maybe we both love her, but I happen to be her husband, and I'm not about to let you break up my family. Got that?"

Miron shook his head. "You have no idea what my life has been like this past year," he told the husband. "Hell. Not even hell, just one great big stale chunk of nothing. And when you've been living with nothing for so long and suddenly something turns up, you can't just tell it to go away. You understand me, don't you? I know you understand me."

The husband bit his lower lip. "If you see her one more time," he said, "I'll kill you. I'm not kidding, and you know it."

"So kill me." Miron shrugged. "That doesn't scare me. We're all going to die in the end."

The husband leaned across the table and socked Miron in the jaw. It was the first time in Miron's life that anyone had hit him so hard. He felt a hot wave of pain surge up somewhere in the middle of his face and spread in every direction. Seconds later, he found himself on the floor, the husband standing over him.

"I'll take her away from here," the husband kept shouting as he went on kicking Miron in the stomach and ribs. "I'll take her far away, to another country, and you won't know where she is. You'll never see her again, you got that, you fucking piece of shit?"

Two waiters jumped on the husband and managed somehow to yank him away. Somebody yelled to the barman to call the police. With his cheek still glued to the coolness of the floor, Miron watched the husband run out of the café. One of the waiters bent over and asked him if he was okay, and Miron made an attempt to answer.

"Do you want me to call an ambulance?" the waiter asked.

Miron whispered that he didn't. "Are you sure?" the waiter insisted. "You're bleeding." Miron nodded slowly and shut his eyes. He tried as hard as he could to imagine himself with that woman. The one he'd never see again. He tried, and for a moment he almost succeeded. His whole body ached. He felt alive.

TEAMWORK

My son wants me to kill her. He's still young and doesn't express this perfectly just yet, but I know exactly what he's after. "I want that Daddy should hit her hard," he says.

"Hard so that she cries?" I ask him.

"No," he says, turning his little head from side to side, "even harder."

He's not violent, my son. He's nearly four and a half, and I can't remember him ever asking me to hit anyone. He's also not the kind of kid who goes around asking for things he doesn't need, like a backpack with a Dora on it or an ice-cream cone. He asks only when he feels he deserves it. Like his father.

And if it's all right to point fingers, then *not* like his mother. Back in the day, she'd roll into the house with tears in her eyes and some story about a guy who'd cursed her on the highway or ripped her off at the store. I'd ask her to go over the specifics three, four different ways, ask questions, investigate down to the tiniest details. Ninety percent of the time it was clear she was at fault. That the guy in the car was right to curse her, and the one at the store—all he did was add the sales tax to her bill.

But my little Roiki isn't like her. And if he asks his father to hit harder than to make her cry, I know there's really something going on. "What'd she do to you?" I ask. "Did she hit you?"

"No," Roiki says. "When Mommy goes out, she babysits me. She locks the door with a key. She leaves me in my room in the dark and won't open it. Even if I cry. Even if I promise to be a good boy."

I hug him tight-tight. "Don't worry," I tell him, "Daddy will make it so Grandma stops."

"You'll hit her harder than hard?" he asks me through tears.

It's plain heartbreaking to see your son cry. Even more when you're divorced. And it fills me with a deep urge to answer Roi with a yes, to swear that I will. But I don't tell Roiki a thing. I'm careful. Because the absolute worst is promising something to a child and not seeing it through. An experience like that scars for life. I straightaway change subjects. I say to him, "Do you want to go to the parking lot at Daddy's work and I'll put you up on my lap and we'll drive the car together—teamwork style?"

As I say *teamwork* his eyes light up, shining with excitement, and the tears that remain from before make them shine even brighter. We drive like that for maybe half an hour in the parking lot, him turning the wheel and me working the pedals. I even let him shift the gears. Reverse cracks him up the most. There's nothing like the laughter of a child.

I bring him back fifteen minutes early. I know they're keeping an eye on us, so I'm extra careful about those things. Before we head up in the elevator I check him twice over to make sure he's looking polished, that I'm delivering him dirt and stain free. Then I give myself the once-over in the lobby mirror, checking for the same things.

"Where were you?" she asks before we're even through the door. "At Gymboree," Roiki answers—exactly as we agreed. "We played with children."

"I hope this time Daddy played nice," Sheyni says, looking all pleased with herself, "and didn't push any kids around."

"Daddy didn't push anyone," I say in a tone that makes it clear I'm not pleased she's baiting me in front of the boy.

"He didn't," Roiki says. "We had a lot of fun!"

He's completely forgotten his crying after the playground, and that he asked me to beat Grandma. That's what's great about kids. Do with them what you will, an hour later they've forgotten all about it and they've found something else to think about, something good to be happy with. But I'm not a kid anymore, and when I get back to the car, all I've got in my head is a picture of Roiki in his tiny room, banging on the door, and that old sour mother of Sheyni's on the other side, not opening it. I have to be smart about this. I need to make sure it stops—but without putting myself in danger and jeopardizing my visits with my son. Even these pathetic biweeklies cost me in blood.

I'm still paying for that one nonincident in the park. A fat little girl attacked Roi in the rope-bridge section. She was pinching him hard and I was just trying to get her away from him. I gave her what is like the absence of a yank, barely pulling at her with my left hand, and the girl—she falls and bangs herself on the metal frame. Nothing, not a scratch, not even enough to get her clearly hysterical mother making a scene. But when Roiki mentions this to Sheyni by accident, she and Amram are suddenly crawling all over me like locusts.

Sheyni says if I have another "violent outburst" in front of the child, the two of them will make sure the agreement we signed finds its way back to court for appeal.

"What violence?" I say to her. "Five years we were together, did I ever once raise a hand?" She knows she's got nothing to say on that front. She had it coming to her a boatload of times, and I was the picture of restraint. A different guy would have kicked her right on over to the emergency room at Ichilov. But me, on my life I'd never raise my hand against a woman. And somehow, before I know it, Amram's gone and got himself involved. "Even now, right this minute, you're violent," is what he throws out at me. "You—you've got a crazy look in your eyes."

"It's not a crazy look," I say, and I smile at him. "It's a touch of the human soul. It's what we call feeling. Just because you have no trace of it in you doesn't mean it's a bad thing."

In the end, springing from the abundance of his nonviolence, it's Amram who starts with the shouting, and the threats, telling me I'll never see my own son again. It's a shame I didn't record him. What a mouth that guy cracked open, filthy as a sewer. But I keep smiling and acting all relaxed just to wind him up. We ended up settling the matter with me promising not to do anything like that ever again. As if it was just exactly what I had scheduled for the next day, to go find myself another five-year-old girl to knock down in the park.

Next time I pick up Roiki from the playground, I go straight for the subject of his grandma. I could wait him out, let him bring it up himself, but children will sit on those kinds of things for a long time, and that's time I don't have. "Since our last talk," I say, "has Grandma come by to babysit you?"

Roiki licks the watermelon ice I bought him and shakes his head. "If she does it again," he asks, "are you going to make Grandma hurt?"

I breathe in. I want more than anything in the world to say yes, but I just can't risk it. If they make it so I can't see him anymore, I'll die. "I want to—more than anything," I tell him. "More than anything in the world, I want to hurt her. To hit her harder than hard. And not just Grandma. The same for anyone who hurts you."

"Like that girl in ice-cream-cone park?" he says, his eyes sparkling.

"Like with the girl from the park." I nod. "But Mommy doesn't like it when Daddy hits. And if Daddy hits Grandma or anyone else, they won't let me come by to play with you anymore. To do all the things we do. Understand?"

Roiki doesn't answer. His Artik drips on his pants. He lets it melt down on purpose, waiting for me to intervene. But I don't. After a long silence, he says, "It's not nice for me alone in the room."

"I know," I tell him, "but I can't make it stop. Only you can. And Daddy wants to teach you how."

I explain to Roiki exactly what to do if his granny locks him in again. Which part of the head he needs to butt against the wall if he wants to leave a solid mark without really injuring himself.

"And it'll hurt?" he asks.

I tell him that it will. I'll never once in this life lie to him. Not like Sheyni. When we were still together, we took Roi to the pediatrician for his vaccinations. The whole way there she was messing with his brain, talking about stings and bees and special treats for good boys, right up until I cut her off mid-sentence and said, "There's going to be a lady there with a needle who's going to cause you pain—but there's nothing we can do about it. There are some things in this world we just have to get on with." And Roiki, who was then barely two, looked at me with that intelligent gaze of his and understood. When we got into the room you could see his whole being wanted to draw back. But he didn't protest and didn't make for the door. He took it like a little man.

Together, we go over every step of the plan. We run through the things he needs to tell Sheyni afterward. How he annoyed Grandma. How she gave him a good shove into the wall. In short, how he got himself that bruise.

"And it'll hurt?" he asks again at the end.

"It'll hurt," I tell him. "Just this once. But afterward, she'll never, not ever, shut you up in that room alone."

Roiki gets quiet. He thinks. The popsicle is already finished. He's licking the stick. "And Mommy won't say that I'm just making it up?"

I stroke his forehead. "If there's a big enough bruise on your head, then, no, she won't say that." After that, we take the car back to the parking lot. Roiki steers, and I press on the gas and the brakes. Teamwork. I teach Roiki how to honk the horn while we drive, and he goes crazy with it. He honks and honks and honks until the parking attendant comes over and asks us to stop. It's this old Arab guy that does the night shift. "Let it slide," I say, winking and holding out a twenty. "The kid's playing. A few more minutes and we're gone." The Arab doesn't say anything. He takes his twenty and starts back toward his booth.

"What'd the man want?" Roiki asks.

"Nothing," I tell him. "He didn't understand where the noise was coming from."

"And I can beep again?"

"Of course you can, angel." I give him a kiss. "More than once. Again and again. Honk until your heart's content."

PUDDING

The whole incident with Avishai Abudi should, in my opinion, set a red light flashing for us all. You'd be hard-pressed to find a more average Joe. He's not the type to go around kicking over garbage pails or starting fights in bars. In fact, he never does anything to set himself apart. And yet, one day, out of nowhere, a pair of thugs are banging at his door. They drag him down the stairs, stick him in the back of some van, and haul him straight to his parents' place. This, with a terrified Avishai in the back yelling, "Who are you? What do you want?"

"That's not what you should be asking," the driver says, and the brute at his side is nodding. "What you mean to say is 'Who am I?' And 'What do I want?'" Afterward the two of them laugh as if Avishai's just told the best joke in the world.

"I'm Avishai Abudi!" Avishai says in a tone intended to sound threatening. "And I want to talk to your superiors. Do you hear me?" That's when the two of them park the van in the lot outside Avishai's parents' building and turn to face him. He's sure they're going to hit him and, also, that he doesn't deserve it. Not at all. "You're in deep," Avishai says, careful to protect his face. "You guys have messed up, big-time!" he says as they pull him out of the van.

But the truth is, they don't beat him at all. Avishai can't see exactly what they're up to, but he senses it. And what he senses is that they are stripping his clothes from him, but not in a sexual way, it's all very proper. After they've finished dressing him back up, they put some sort of heavy pack on his back and say, "Hurry up, run along home to Mommy and Daddy. You wouldn't want to be late." And Avishai runs. He runs as fast as he possibly can. He takes the stairs three at a time, until he reaches the brown wooden door to his parents' apartment. He knocks on it, panting, and when Mommy opens the door, he hurries inside, closes it behind him, and double locks it. "What's gotten into you?" Mommy asks. "Why are you sweating like that."

"I ran," Avishai pants, "in the stairwell. People. Don't open."

"I don't understand a thing," Mommy says, "but never mind. Come, put your bag down and go wash your hands and face. Dinner's already on the table." Avishai takes off the knapsack, goes into the bathroom, and washes his face. In the mirror over the sink he sees that he's in his school uniform. When he opens the knapsack in the living room he discovers notebooks and textbooks lined in flowered paper. There's a math book, and a box of colored pencils, and a little metal compass with an eraser shoved on the point. His mother comes over to chide him. "This isn't the time for homework. Come and eat. Hurry up, chop-chop, before all the vitamins escape from the salad." Avishai sits at the table and eats in silence. The food is delicious. He'd been surviving solely on takeout and cheap restaurants for so many years, he'd honestly forgotten that food could taste this good. "Daddy left you money for your after-school program." Mommy points to a sealed white envelope resting on the little hall table next to the rotary phone. "But I'm warning you, Avi, if you pull the same stunt you did with the model-airplane club and change your mind after one class, you're better off telling us now, before we pay."

Avishai thinks to himself: It's just a dream. And after that he says, "Yes, Mommy," because even if it is just a dream, there's no need to be impolite. He thinks to himself: If I just will it, I can wake myself at any moment. Not that he knows what, exactly, you do to wake up in the middle of a dream. You can pinch yourself, but that's generally used in the opposite situation. Pinching is what you do to prove you're already awake. Maybe he could hold his breath, or just say to himself, "Wake up! Wake up!" And maybe if he simply refuses to absorb everything around him, if he casts doubt, it'll all suddenly melt away. In either case, there's no need to stress. He might as well eat first. Yes, after dinner is probably an excellent time to wake himself up. And when Avishai really gets to thinking about it, even when he's done eating, it's not exactly urgent. He can go to his after-school group first—he's honestly curious which one it is—and later, if it's still light out, he can play a little soccer in the schoolyard. And only when Daddy gets home from work, only then will he wake up. He could even stretch it out another day or two, until right before some especially hard exam. "Now what are you daydreaming about?" Mommy asks, stroking his balding head. "So many thoughts spinning around behind those big, round eyes of yours, just looking at them makes me feel tired."

"I was thinking of dessert," Avishai lies, "wondering if you'd made Jell-O or chocolate pudding."

"What would you like there to be?" Mommy asks.

"Pudding," Avishai says, all playful.

"It's already waiting," his mother says happily and opens the fridge. "But if you change your mind, Jell-O is just as easy. It won't take a minute to make."

UNZIPPING

It began with a kiss. It almost always begins with a kiss. Ella and Tsiki were in bed, naked, with only their tongues touching—when she felt something prick her. "Did I hurt you?" Tsiki asked, and when she shook her head, he quickly added, "You're bleeding." And she was, from the mouth. "I'm sorry," he said, and he started a frantic search in the kitchen, pulling ice-cube trays out of the freezer and banging them against the counter. "Here, take these," he said, handing her some ice with a shivering hand, "put them against your lip. It'll stop the bleeding." Tsiki had always been good at those things. In the army he'd been a paramedic. He was a trained tour guide too. "I'm sorry," he went on, turning paler, "I must have bitten you. You know, in the heat of passion." "Never——ind." She smiled at him, the ice cube sticking to her lower lip. "No——ing ha——ened." Which was a lie, of course. Because some——ing had ha——ened. It isn't every day that someone you're living with makes you bleed, and then lies to you and says he bit you, when you distinctly felt something pricking you.

They didn't kiss for a few days after that, because of her cut. Lips are a very sensitive part of the body. And later, when they could, they had to be very careful. She could tell he was hiding something. And sure enough, one night, taking advantage of the fact that he slept with his mouth open, she gently slipped her finger under his tongue—and found it. It was a zipper. A teensy zipper. But when she pulled at it, her whole Tsiki opened up like an oyster, and inside was Jurgen. Unlike Tsiki, Jurgen had a goatee, meticulously shaped sideburns, and an uncircumcised penis. Ella watched him in his sleep. Very, very quietly she folded up the Tsiki wrapping and hid it in the kitchen cabinet behind the trash can, where they kept the garbage bags.

Life with Jurgen wasn't easy. The sex was fantastic, but he drank a lot, and when he did, he'd make a racket and get into all kinds of embarrassing situations. On top of that, he liked to make her feel guilty for being the reason he'd left Europe and come to live here. Whenever anything bad happened in this country, whether it was in real life or on TV, he'd say to her, "Look what your country is coming to." His Hebrew was lousy, and that "your" of his always sounded very accusatory. Her parents didn't like him. Her mother, who had actually been fond of Tsiki, called Jurgen the goy. Her father would always ask him about work, and Jurgen would snigger and say, "Work is like a mustache, Mr. Shviro. It went out of style a long time ago." Which nobody ever found amusing, certainly not Ella's father, who still happened to sport a mustache.

Finally, Jurgen left. He went back to Düsseldorf to make music and live on benefits. He'd never be able to make it as a singer in this country, he said, because they'd hold his accent against him. People here were prejudiced. They didn't like Germans. Ella thought that even in Germany his weird music and kitschy lyrics wouldn't really get him very far. He'd even written a song about her. It was called "Goddess" and the whole thing was about having sex on the breakwater and about how when she came, it was "like a wave breaking against a rock"—and that's a quote.

Six months after Jurgen left she was looking for a garbage bag and found the Tsiki wrapping. Maybe it had been a mistake to open his zipper, she thought. Could be. With things like that it's hard to say for sure. That same evening, while she was brushing her teeth, she thought back over that kiss, over the pain of being pricked. She rinsed her mouth with lots of water and looked in the mirror. She still had a scar, and when she studied it up close, she noticed a little zipper under her tongue. Ella fingered it hesitantly, and tried to imagine what she'd be like inside. It made her very hopeful, but also a little worried—mainly about freckled hands and a dry complexion. Maybe she'd have a tattoo, she thought, of a rose. She'd always wanted to have one, but never had the nerve. She'd thought it would hurt a lot.

THE POLITE LITTLE BOY

The polite little boy knocked on the door. His parents were too busy fighting to answer, and after he'd knocked a few times he went in anyway. "A mistake," the father said to the mother, "that's what we are, a mistake, like in those pictures where they show you how not to do something. That's what we are, with a big 'No!' underneath and the face crossed out with a big X." "What do you want me to say?" the mother said to the father. "I mean, anything I say now I'll regret later." "Say it, say it," the father snarled. "Why wait till later when you can regret it right now?" The polite little boy had a model airplane in his hand. He'd built it himself. The instructions were in a language he didn't understand, but there were good drawings, with arrows, and the polite little boy, whose father always said he had good hands, managed to figure them out and to build the model airplane, with no help from grownups. "I used to laugh," the mother said, "I'd laugh a lot, every day. And now . . ." She stroked the polite little boy's hair distractedly. "I don't anymore, that's all." "That's all?" the father roared. "That's all? That's your 'I'll regret saying it later': 'I used to laugh'? Big fucking deal!"

"What a nice plane," the mother said, and she very deliberately turned her gaze away from the father. "Why don't you go outside and play with it?" "May I?" the polite little boy asked. "Of course you may." The mother smiled and stroked his hair again, the way you stroke a dog's head. "And how long may I stay outside?" the polite little boy asked. "As long as you want," the father blurted, "and if you like it out there, you don't have to come back at all. Just pick up the phone from time to time, so Mother doesn't worry." The mother got up and slapped the father as hard as she could. It was strange, because it looked as if this slap only made the father happy, and it was actually the mother who started crying. "Go on, go ahead," the mother told the polite little boy between her sobs, "Go out and play, while there's still light outside, but be back before it gets dark." Maybe his face is hard as a stone, the polite little boy thought to himself as he walked down the stairs, and that's why it hurts your hand when you hit it.

The polite little boy threw the model airplane in the air as high as he could. It made a loop, went on gliding a little in parallel with the ground, and bumped into a drinking fountain. The wing was a little bent out of shape and the polite little boy tried hard to straighten it. "Wow," said a freckle-faced little girl he hadn't noticed until then, and she held out her freckled hand. "What a cool plane. Can I fly it too?" "It isn't a plane," the little boy corrected. "It's a model airplane. A plane is only if it has a motor." "C'mon, let me try it," the little girl ordered without lowering her hand. "Don't be mean." "I have to fix the wing first," the little boy stalled. "Can't you see it's bent out of shape?" "You're mean," the little girl said. "I hope lots of horrible things happen to you." She wrinkled her forehead, trying to think of something more specific, and when it came to her, she smiled: "I hope your mommy dies. That's it, I hope she dies. Amen." The polite little boy paid no attention to her, just like he'd been taught to do. He was a head taller than the little girl and if he'd wanted to he could have slapped her, and it would have hurt the little girl a lot, much more than it would have hurt him, because her freckled face was definitely not made of stone. But he didn't, and he didn't kick her either, or throw a pebble, or swear back at her, because he was polite. "And I hope your daddy dies too," the little girl added, as if it were an afterthought, and walked away.

The polite little boy flew the model airplane a few more times. On his best throw, it made three whole loops in the air before dropping to the ground. The sun was beginning to drop too, and the sky all around was getting redder and redder. His father had told him once that if you look at the sun for a very long time without blinking, you can go blind, and that's why the polite little boy was careful to close his eyes every few seconds. But even with his eyes closed, he could still see the redness of the sky. It was strange, and the polite little boy was very eager to understand it a little better, but he knew that unless he got home on time, his mother would worry. "The sun always rises," the polite little boy thought to himself, and bent over to pick up the model airplane off the lawn, "and I'm never late."

When the polite little boy went indoors, his mother was still in the living room crying, clutching her hand. The father wasn't there. She said he was in their bedroom, asleep, because he was doing a night shift, and she went to make the polite little boy his scrambled supper. The bedroom door was ajar and the polite little boy gave it a gentle push. The father was lying on the bed with his shoes and his street clothes on.

He was on his stomach with his eyes open, and when the polite little boy peeked inside, he asked without lifting his head up off the bed, "How's the model airplane?" "It's okay," the polite little boy said, and when he felt that what he'd said wasn't enough, he added, "It's really okay." "Mother and I fight sometimes and say things to hurt one another," the father said, looking down at the floor and then at him, "but you know that I'll always love you. Always. No matter what anyone says. Don't you?" "Yes." The polite little boy nodded and started closing the door behind him. "I know. Thank you."

MYSTIQUE

The man who knew what I was about to say sat next to me on the plane, a stupid smile plastered across his face. That's what was so nerve-racking about him, the fact that he wasn't smart or even sensitive, and yet he knew the lines and managed to say them—all the lines I meant to say—three seconds before me. "D'you sell Guerlain Mystique?" he asked the flight attendant a minute before I could, and she gave him an orthodontic smile and said there was just one last bottle left. "My wife's crazy about that perfume. It's like an addiction with her. If I come back from a trip and don't pick up a bottle of Mystique from duty-free, she tells me I don't love her anymore. If I dare walk in the door without at least one bottle, I'm in trouble." That was supposed to be my line, but the man who knew what I was about to say stole it from me. He didn't miss a beat. As soon as the wheels touched down, he switched on his cell phone, a second before I did, and called his wife. "I just landed," he told her. "I'm sorry. I know it was supposed to be yesterday. They canceled the flight. You don't believe me? Check it out yourself. Call Eric. I know you don't. I can give you his number right now." I also have a travel agent called Eric. He'd lie for me too.

When the plane reached the gate he was still on the

phone, giving all the answers I would have given. Without a trace of emotion, like a parrot in a world where time flows backwards, repeating whatever's about to be said instead of what's been said already. His answers were the best possible, under the circumstances. His circumstances weren't so hot, not so hot at all. Mine weren't all that great either. My wife hadn't taken my call yet, but just listening to the man who knew what I was about to say made me want to hang up. Just listening to him I could tell that the hole I was in was so deep that if I ever managed to dig myself out, it would be to a different reality. She'd never forgive me, she'd never trust me. Ever. From now on, every trip would be hell on earth, and the time in between would be even worse. He went on and on and on, delivering all those sentences that I'd thought up and hadn't said yet. They just kept flowing out of him. Now he stepped it up, raising his voice, like a drowning man desperate to stay afloat. People started filing out of the plane. He got up, still talking, scooped up his laptop in his other hand, and headed for the exit. I could see him leaving it behind, the bag he'd stashed in the overhead compartment. I could see him forgetting it, and I didn't say anything. I just stayed put. Gradually, the plane emptied, till the only ones left were an overweight religious woman with a million children, and me. I got up and opened the overhead compartment, like it was the most natural thing in the world to do. I took out the duty-free bag, like it had always been mine. Inside were the receipt and the bottle of Guerlain Mystique. My wife's crazy about that perfume. It's like an addiction with her. If I come back from a trip and don't pick up a bottle of Mystique from duty-free, she tells me I don't love her anymore. If I dare walk in the door without at least one bottle, I'm in trouble.

CREATIVE WRITING

The first story Maya wrote was about a world in which people split themselves in two instead of reproducing. In that world, every person could, at any given moment, turn into two beings, each half his/her age. Some chose to do this when they were young; for instance, an eighteen-year-old might split into two nine-year-olds. Others would wait until they'd established themselves professionally and financially and go for it only in middle age. The heroine of Maya's story was splitless. She had reached the age of eighty and, despite all the social pressure, insisted on not splitting. At the end of the story, she died.

It was a good story, except for the ending. There was something depressing about that part, Aviad thought. Depressing and predictable. But in the writing workshop she had signed up for, Maya actually got a lot of compliments on the ending. The instructor, who was supposed to be this well-known writer, even though Aviad had never heard of him, told her that there was something soul-piercing about the banality of the ending, or some other piece of crap. Aviad saw how happy that compliment made Maya. She was very excited when she told him about it. She recited what the writer had said to her the way people recite a verse from the Bible. And Aviad, who had originally tried to suggest a different ending, backpedaled and said that it was all a matter of taste and that he really didn't understand much about it.

It had been her mother's idea that she should go to a creative writing workshop. She'd said that a friend's daughter had attended one and enjoyed it very much. Aviad also thought it would be good for Maya to get out more, to do something with herself. He could always bury himself in work, but since the miscarriage, she never left the house. Whenever he came home he found her in the living room, sitting up straight on the couch. Not reading, not watching TV, not even crying. When Maya hesitated about the course, Aviad knew how to persuade her. "Go once, give it a try," he said, "the way a kid goes to day camp." Later he realized that it had been a little insensitive of him to use a child as an example after what they'd been through two months before. But Maya actually smiled and said that day camp might be just what she needed.

The second story she wrote was about a world in which you could see only the people you loved. The protagonist was a married man in love with his wife. One day, his wife walked right into him in the hallway and the glass he was holding fell and shattered on the floor. A few days later, she sat down on him as he was dozing in an armchair. Both times, she wriggled out of it with an excuse: she'd had something else on her mind; she hadn't been looking when she sat down. But the husband started to suspect that she didn't love him anymore. To test his theory, he decided to do something drastic: he shaved off the left side of his mustache. He came home with half a mustache, clutching a bouquet of anemones. His wife thanked him for the flowers and smiled. He could sense her groping the air as she tried to give him a kiss. Maya called the story "Half a Mustache," and told Aviad that when she had read it aloud in the workshop, some people cried. Aviad said, "Wow," and kissed her on the forehead. That night, they fought about some stupid little thing. She'd forgotten to pass on a message or something like that, and he yelled at her. He was to blame, and in the end he apologized. "I had a hellish day at work," he said, and he stroked her leg, trying to make up for his outburst, "Do you forgive me?" She forgave him.

The workshop instructor had published a novel and a collection of short stories. Neither had been much of a success, but they'd had a few good reviews. At least, that's what the saleswoman at a bookstore near Aviad's office told him. The novel was very thick, 624 pages. Aviad bought the book of short stories. He kept it in his desk and tried to read a little during lunch breaks. Each story in the collection took place in a different country. It was a kind of gimmick. The blurb on the back cover said that the writer had worked for years as a tour guide and had traveled in Cuba and Africa and that his travels had influenced his writing. There was also a small black-and-white photograph of him. In it, he had the kind of smug smile of someone who feels lucky to be who he is. The writer had told Maya, she said to Aviad, that when the workshop was over, he'd send her stories to his editor. And, although she shouldn't get her hopes up, publishers these days were desperate for new talent.

Her third story started out funny. It was about a pregnant woman who gave birth to a cat. The hero of the story was the husband, who suspected that the cat wasn't his. A fat ginger tomcat that slept on the lid of the dumpster right below the window of the couple's bedroom gave the husband a condescending look every time he went downstairs to throw out the garbage. In the end, there was a violent clash between the husband and the cat. The husband threw a stone at the cat, who countered with bites and scratches. The injured husband, his wife, and the kitten she was breastfeeding went to the clinic for him to get a rabies shot. He was humiliated and in pain, but tried not to cry while they were waiting. The kitten, sensing his suffering, curled itself from its mother's embrace, went over to him, and licked his face tenderly, offering a consoling "Meow."

"Did you hear that?" the mother asked emotionally. "He said 'Daddy.'"

At that point, the husband could no longer hold back his tears. And when Aviad read that passage, he had to try hard not to cry too. Maya said that she'd started writing the story even before she knew she was pregnant again. "Isn't it weird," she asked, "how my brain didn't know yet, but my subconscious did?"

The next Tuesday, when Aviad was supposed to pick her up after the workshop, he arrived half an hour early, parked his car in the lot, and went to find her. Maya was surprised to see him in the classroom, and he insisted that she introduce him to the writer. The writer reeked of body lotion. He shook Aviad's hand limply and told him that if Maya had chosen him for a husband, he must be a very special person.

Three weeks later, Aviad signed up for a beginner's creative writing class. He didn't say anything about it to Maya, and to be on the safe side, he told his secretary that if he had any calls from home, she should say that he was in an important meeting and couldn't be disturbed. The other members of the class were elderly women, who gave him dirty looks. The thin, young instructor wore a headscarf, and the women in the class gossiped about her, saying that she lived in a settlement in the occupied territories and had cancer. She asked everyone to do an exercise in automatic writing. "Write whatever comes into your head," she said. "Don't think, just write." Aviad tried to stop thinking. It was very hard. The old women around him wrote with nervous speed, like students racing to finish an exam before the teacher tells them to put their pens down, and after a few minutes, he began writing too.

The story he wrote was about a fish that was swimming happily along in the sea when a wicked witch turned it into a man. The fish couldn't come to terms with his transformation and decided to chase down the wicked witch and make her turn him back into a fish. Since he was an especially quick and enterprising fish, he managed to get married while he was pursuing her, and even to establish a small company that imported plastic products from the Far East. With the help of the enormous knowledge he had gained as a fish that had crossed the seven seas, the company began to thrive and even went public. Meanwhile, the wicked witch, who was a little tired after all her years of wickedness, decided to find all the people and creatures she'd cast spells on, apologize to them, and restore them to their natural state. At one point, she even went to see the fish she had turned into a man. The fish's secretary asked her to wait until he'd finished a satellite meeting with his partners in Taiwan. At that stage in his life, the fish could hardly remember that he was in fact a fish, and his company now controlled half the world. The witch waited several hours, but when she saw that the meeting wouldn't be ending anytime soon, she climbed onto her broom and flew off. The fish kept doing better and better, until one day, when he was really old, he looked out the window of one of the dozens of huge shoreline buildings he'd purchased in a smart real estate deal, and saw the sea. And suddenly he remembered that he was a fish. A very rich fish who controlled many subsidiary companies that were traded on stock markets around the world, but still a fish. A fish who, for years, had not tasted the salt of the sea.

When the instructor saw that Aviad had put down his pen, she gave him an inquiring look. "I don't have an ending," he whispered apologetically, keeping his voice down so as not to disturb the old ladies who were still writing.

SNOT

A father and son are sitting at a desk in an acupuncturist's treatment room, waiting.

The acupuncturist comes in.

He's Chinese.

He sits down behind the desk.

In strangely accented English, he asks the son to put his hands on the desk.

The Chinese acupuncturist puts his fingers on the son's arms and closes his eyes, then asks the son to stick out his tongue.

The son sticks it out defiantly.

The Chinese acupuncturist nods and asks the son to lie down on the treatment bed.

The son lies down on the bed and closes his eyes.

The father asks if the son should take off his clothes.

The acupuncturist shakes his head.

He takes some long, thin needles out of his desk drawer and starts sticking them into the son.

One behind each ear.

One in each cheek, close to the nose.

One on each side of his forehead, close to the eye.

The son moans quietly, his eyes still closed.

Now, says the acupuncturist to father and son, we have to wait.

And after the treatment, asks the father, will he feel better?

The acupuncturist shrugs and walks out.

The father goes over to the bed and puts a hand on his son's shoulder.

The son's body contracts.

The son didn't flinch when his skin was being pierced by needles, but he does now. Half an hour later, the Chinese acupuncturist comes back and pulls each needle out with a swift movement.

He tells the father and the son that the boy's body is responding to the treatment, and that's a good sign.

As proof, he points to the spots where the needles had been inserted. There is a red circle around each one.

Then he sits down behind the desk.

The father asks how much the treatment costs.

He'd planned to ask before the treatment, but forgot. If he'd remembered to ask earlier, he would have had a better bargaining position. Not that he planned to bargain. After all, we're talking about the health of his only son here. His only living son, that is.

The acupuncturist says 350 shekels per treatment and then tells him that there is medication the son has to take after eating, and that costs another hundred.

The acupuncturist explains that the boy needs a series of treatments. At least ten. Every day except Saturday.

The acupuncturist adds that it would be better if they could do the treatment on Saturday too, but he doesn't work Saturdays because his wife won't let him.

Wife is almost the only word other than *snot* that he says in Hebrew.

When he says *wife*, the father feels a terrible sense of loneliness.

Then the father has a strange idea.

He wants to tell the acupuncturist that he has to use the bathroom, and then, after locking the door behind him, he'll masturbate into the toilet.

He thinks this will bring him some relief from that sense of loneliness. He's not sure.

In Chinese medicine, sperm is considered a form of energy. When you ejaculate it, you are weakened, and that's why it isn't recommended. Especially when you're weak to begin with.

The father doesn't know any of that, but he gives up on the idea anyway. Loneliness is hard for him, but he doesn't feel comfortable leaving his son alone with the Chinese acupuncturist.

Every day except Saturday, the acupuncturist repeats. He thinks the father wasn't listening the first time.

The father pays with new bills. Exactly 450. No change necessary.

They make an appointment for the next day.

On the way to the door, the Chinese acupuncturist says in Hebrew, "Be well, you two."

The son thinks it's weird for the acupuncturist to say that. After all, he's the only one who's sick.

The father doesn't notice it. He's thinking about something else.

Wife; snot; Be well, you two.

Be well, you two; snot; wife.

There's nothing stranger than hearing a Chinese man speak Hebrew.

GRAB THE CUCKOO BY THE TAIL

It's hardest at night. Don't get me wrong, though. I'm not say-ing I miss her most at night—because I don't miss her, period. But at night, when I'm alone in bed, I do think about her. Not warm, fuzzy thoughts about all the good moments we had. More like a picture of her in panties and a T-shirt, sleep-ing with her mouth open, breathing heavily, leaving a circle of saliva on the pillow, and of myself watching her. What did I actually feel then when I was watching her? First of all, amazement that I wasn't turned off, and after that, a sort of affection. Not love. Affection. The kind you feel toward an animal or a baby more than toward a wife. Then I cry. Almost every night. And not out of regret. I have nothing to regret. She's the one who left. And looking back, our splitting up was good, not just for her, for both of us. And it's even better that we did it before there were kids in the middle to make everything more complicated. So why do I cry? Because that's just how it is. When something gets taken away from you, even if it's shit, it hurts. When a tumor is removed, you're left with a scar. And the best time to scratch it seems to be at night.

Uzi has a new cell phone, the kind that gets real-time updates from the stock market. When the stocks of his computer company go up, his cell plays "Simply the Best," and when they go down, it plays "A Hard Rain's a-Gonna Fall." He's been walking around with that cell for a month now, and it makes him laugh every time. "Simply the Best" makes him laugh more than "A Hard Rain's a-Gonna Fall," because, after all, it's easier to laugh when money is pouring down on you than when someone is snatching it out of your wallet. And today, Uzi tells me, is a big day because he's planning to invest a bundle in NASDAQ options. Those options are called QQQQ, but Uzi thinks it's funnier to call them "cuckoo." If the NASDAQ goes up, so do they. And since the NASDAQ, according to Uzi, is going to fly through the ceiling any minute, all we have to do is grab the cuckoo by the tail and fly with it to the sky.

It takes Uzi twenty minutes to explain this, and when he's finished, he checks his cell-phone display again. When he began his explanation, the cuckoo was 1.3, and now it's already 1.55. "We suck," Uzi laments as he chews his almond croissant, spraying crumbs every which way. "Do you realize that in just this last half hour, we could have made more than ten percent on our money?"

"Why do you keep saying *we*?" I ask. "And what money are you talking about? You think I have money to put into this thing?"

"You don't have to put in a lot," Uzi says. "If we'd put in five thousand, we'd be five hundred ahead. But we didn't. You know what? Forget it, why am I making you a part of this? I didn't. And that's even though, deep down, I knew for an absolute fact—the way a baby knows that his mother will always love him—that NASDAQ would break 1.5."

"There are mothers who abandon their babies," I say.

"Maybe," Uzi mumbles, "but not the cuckoo's mother. I'm telling you, I should have put all my money on it, but I decided to wait. And you know why? Because I'm a loser."

"You're not . . ." I try, but Uzi's too far into it to stop. "Look at me, I'm thirty-five and I don't even have a million."

"But just a week ago you told me you invested more than a million in the market," I say.

"Shekels," Uzi snorts contemptuously. "What's a million shekels? I'm talking dollars here." Uzi swallows the last piece of croissant sadly and washes it down with a swig of Diet Coke. "Look around," he says. "Pimple-faced kids who served me coffee in Styrofoam cups at start-ups created by me are driving BMWs while I drive a Peugeot 205 like some dental hygienist."

"Stop whining," I tell him. "Believe me, a lot of people would kill to trade places with you."

"A lot of people?" Uzi laughed to himself, half maliciously. "A lot of which people? A lot of the jobless in Sderot? A lot of lepers in India? What's with you, Dedi? You've turned Amish on me now? Looks to me like that divorce fucked you up completely."

Uzi and I have known each other since we were about three. A lot of time has passed since then, but not a lot has changed. Uzi says that even then I felt sorry for myself all the time. When we were in high school, I fantasized about a girl-friend while Uzi was already trying to make a killing. He started a summer camp for kids. His business plan was simple: the money he got from the parents he split fifty-fifty with the kids, and in return, the kids didn't snitch on him for not organizing any activities except for tossing a ratty soccer ball on the grass for them to kick around and letting them drink from the water fountain once every two hours. Today Uzi has his own apartment, a wife who was once a secretary in some bubble company he worked for, and a chubby little daughter who looks just like him. "If we get divorced now," Uzi says, "she gets half. Of everything. And it's all because I was a pussy before the wedding and didn't make her sign a prenup."

I've already paid for breakfast and now we're waiting for the change. "You, on the other hand," Uzi continues, "came out of your divorce like a champ. She didn't take a shekel."

"That's because there was nothing to take." I try to put the compliment into perspective.

"For the time being"—Uzi pats me on the back—"for the time being. And now that the whole business between the two of you is signed and sealed, this is the perfect time to strike and be the only winner, like in the one-winner sweep-stakes, without partners."

"Without partners," I repeat automatically, and swallow the last, sweetest drops of my coffee.

"Without partners," Uzi repeats, "just me and you. I have a feeling that the cuckoo is going to drop a little again, not really low, to maybe one point three five, and then we buy. We buy the pants off it." The waitress doesn't come back with the change. The owner walks over instead. "Excuse me," he says, "I'm very sorry to bother you, but the hundred-shekel bill you gave the waitress is counterfeit. Look." He holds the bill up to the light. "It's not real." I take the bill and look at the watermark. Instead of a drawing of former president ben Zvi, a scribbled smiley face looks out at me.

"Counterfeit?" Uzi snatches the bill out of my hand. "Let me see," he says, and tosses the owner a different bill, which he examines against the light too. Meanwhile, I apologize. "I took a taxi here and paid the driver with a two-hundred-shekel bill," I tell the owner. "He must have palmed the fake bill off on me as change."

"This bill, it's so cool," Uzi says. "Will you sell it to me? For a hundred?"

"What are you so excited about?" I ask Uzi. "It's counterfeit."

"That's why, you idiot," Uzi says, and takes a bundle of bills out of his wallet. "Noncounterfeits I already have. But counterfeit is classy. I'll dump it on anyone who gives me shitty service."

"Okay," I say, "so take it. A counterfeit hundred as a gift from me."

Now we're in Uzi's car. We just got in. I don't know why I told him that I cry at night. Uzi is not exactly the person to share stuff like that with. "And it's not because of her," I stress. "I don't want her to come back."

"Yeah, I know," Uzi mumbles, "I know her." His cell phone tells him he's simply the best, but he doesn't even glance at the display to see how much the stock went up, he just moves his face right up to mine and stares at me from an inch away like a doctor examining a patient. "You know what you need, and right now?" he says. "An Ethiopian sandwich at Fifty-six Matalon Street."

"We just ate," I protest.

"A sandwich isn't food," Uzi says, fiddling with the steering-wheel lock, "a sandwich is one Ethiopian chick under you and another one on top of you, pressing her tits into your back. I gotta tell you that when I first heard about it, it didn't turn me on either, but it really is something."

"What's Fifty-six Matalon Street?" I ask. "A whorehouse?"

"Let's not change the subject," Uzi says, turning on the ignition, "we're talking about you now. You haven't fucked even once since you and Ofra split, right?"

I nod and say, "And I don't feel like it either."

"In life"—Uzi releases the hand brake—"you don't always do what you feel like."

"If you're trying to tell me that I cry because I'm not fucking, then you're wrong," I object.

"I'm not saying that"—Uzi drums the wheel with his fingers—"I'm saying that you cry because your life is empty. Because it has no meaning. And when you're empty inside . . ." He touches himself on the chest slightly to the right of his heart. "If there's meaning around you, you put some of it inside yourself, and if there isn't, you shove in a plug. Just for the time being, till the manufacturer sends along the meaning. And in cases like that, an Ethiopian sandwich is a great plug."

"Take me home," I say. "My life is pathetic enough without going to whores." But Uzi isn't with me anymore. His cell phone is ringing again with an unfamiliar, boring ringtone programmed for incoming calls. It's someone from the bank. Uzi tells him to buy $20,000 of the QQQQ, which has gone down again. "Ten thousand for me and another ten thousand for a friend."

I shake my head at him, but Uzi ignores me. And when he hangs up he says, "Get used to it, Dedi, you and me, we're gonna grab the cuckoo by the tail."

Through the thin wall I can hear Uzi's cell sing to him that he's simply the best and a woman roaring with laughter. There were no Ethiopians at 56 Matalon Street today, so Uzi went into a room with a big-boobed girl who said in English that she was Czech, and I had a bleach blonde, probably Russian. On the other side of the wall, Uzi is laughing out loud now too—I guess a Czech open sandwich isn't a bad plug either. The blonde's name is Maria, and she asks me if I want her to help me get undressed. I tell her that won't be necessary, that I'm there only because of my crazy friend and that as far as I'm concerned, we can just sit there together till Uzi finishes and then leave, without fucking. "No fuck?" Maria tries to understand. "Suck?" On the other side of the wall, Uzi's cell keeps telling him he's simply the best. Something good is happening in there. Maria unbuttons my pants and I tell myself that if I ask her to stop, she'll be insulted. I know that isn't true, but I make an effort to believe it. Maybe Uzi is right and all I need now is a plug. While she's doing it, I try to invent a life for her, a happy one that brought her to prostitution out of choice. I once saw a movie like that, about a cheerful, bighearted French whore. Maybe Maria's that way too, only Russian. When I look down, all I can see is her hair. Every once in a while she raises her head and asks, "Is good?" and I nod in embarrassment. Soon it'll be over.

During the half hour we spend at 56 Matalon Street, the cuckoo flies right through the ceiling. By the time we're back on the sunbaked street, it has already reached 1.75, which according to Uzi, gives us 100 percent on our money. And so the cuckoo continues to slice through the blue sky like a kite, with us right behind it, clutching its tail tightly, trying not to fall.

PICK A COLOR

A black man moved into a white neighborhood. He had a black house with a black porch where he used to sit every morning and drink his black coffee, until one black night, his white neighbors came into his house and beat the crap out of him. He lay there curled up like an umbrella handle in a pool of black blood and they kept on beating him, until one of them started yelling that they should stop because if he died on them they might end up in prison.

The black man didn't die on them. An ambulance came and took him far, far away to an enchanted hospital on the top of an inactive volcano. The hospital was white. Its gates were white, the walls of its rooms were white, and so was the bedding. The black man began to recover. Recover and fall in love. Fall in love with a white nurse in a white uniform who took care of him with great devotion and kindness. She loved him too. And like him, that love of theirs grew stronger with every passing day, grew stronger and learned to get out of bed and crawl. Like a small child. Like a baby. Like a black man who had been badly beaten.

They got married in a yellow church. A yellow priest married them. His yellow parents had come to that country on a yellow ship. They had been beaten up by their white neighbors too. But he didn't get into all that with the black man. He barely knew him, and anyway, he didn't want to go there, what with the ceremony and everything. He planned to say that God loves them and wishes them all the best. The yellow man didn't know that for sure. He'd tried lots of times to convince himself that he did. That he knows that God loves everyone and wishes us all only the best. But that day, when he married that battered black man, not even thirty and already covered with scars and sitting in a wheelchair, it was harder for him to believe. "God loves you both," he finally said anyway. "God loves you and wishes you all the best," he said, and was ashamed.

The black man and the white woman lived together happily, until one day, when the woman was walking home from the grocery store, a brown man with a brown knife who was waiting for her in the stairwell told her to give him everything she had. When the black man came home, he found her dead. He didn't understand why the brown man had stabbed her, because he could have just taken her money and run. The funeral service took place in the yellow priest's yellow church, and when the black man saw the yellow priest, he grabbed him by his yellow robe and said, "But you told us. You told us that God loves us. If he loves us, why did he do such a terrible thing to us?" The yellow priest had a ready-made answer. An answer they'd taught him in priest school; something about God working in mysterious ways and that now that the woman was dead, she was surely closer to Him. But instead of using that answer, the priest began cursing. He cursed God viciously. Insulting and hurtful curses the likes of which had never been heard in the world before. Curses so insulting and hurtful that even God was offended.

God entered the yellow church on the disabled ramp. He was in a wheelchair too; He had once lost a woman too. He was silvery. Not the cheap, glittery silver of a banker's BMW, but a muted, matte silver. Once, as He was gliding among the silvery stars with his silvery beloved, a gang of golden gods attacked them. When they were kids, God had once beaten one of them up, a short, skinny golden god who had now grown up and returned with his friends. The golden gods beat Him with golden clubs of sunlight and didn't stop until they'd broken every bone in His divine body. It took Him years to recuperate. His beloved never did. She remained a vegetable. She could see and hear everything, but she couldn't say a word. The silvery God decided to create a species in His own image so she could watch it to pass the time. That species really did resemble Him: battered and victimized like Him. And His silvery beloved stared wide-eyed at the members of that species for hours, stared and didn't even shed a tear.

"What do you think," the silvery God asked the yellow priest in frustration, "that I created all of you like this because it's what I wanted? Because I'm some kind of pervert or sadist who enjoys all this suffering? I created you like this because this is what I know. It's the best I can do."

The yellow priest fell to his knees and begged His forgiveness. If a stronger God had come to his church, he probably would have carried on cursing him, even if he had to go to hell for it. But seeing the silvery, disabled God made him feel regret and sorrow, and he really did want His forgiveness. The black man didn't fall to his knees. With the bottom half of his body paralyzed, he couldn't do things like that anymore. He just sat in his wheelchair and pictured a silvery goddess somewhere in the heavens looking down at him with gaping eyes. That imbued him with a sense of purpose, of hope, even. He couldn't explain to himself exactly why, but the thought that he was suffering just like a god made him feel blessed.

BLACK AND BLUE

In the ER they said the bone was fractured and the muscle was nearly torn in two places. Some people, the doctor said, can walk away from a fifty-mile-an-hour head-on collision without a scratch. Once there was this man who arrived in the ER, a fat guy who'd fallen out of his third-floor apartment onto the asphalt, and all he had was a black-and-blue mark on his backside. It's all a matter of luck. Which she, apparently, didn't have much of. One wrong move on her way down the stairs, an ankle that turned the wrong way—and here she was, in the hospital, with a cast.

A guy who looked like an Arab wrapped the wet bandages around her foot. He told her he was just an intern and that if she wanted, she could wait for the doctor to do it, but it would take at least another hour, because they had a backlog. When he'd finished with the cast, he told her that because it was summer, it would itch all the time. He didn't give her any tips on what to do about this, just the bottom line. A few minutes later, it really did begin to itch.

If it hadn't been for the cast, she wouldn't have been home when David phoned. If it hadn't been for the cast, she would have been at work. He told her he was in Tel Aviv, he'd come to Israel just for a week, to attend some conference, something to do with the Jewish Agency. He said he was wasting away in those lectures and he wanted to see her, and she said okay. If it hadn't been for the cast, she'd have made some excuse and talked her way out of it, but she was bored. If he came, she thought, there would be the excitement leading up to it. She'd stand in front of the mirror and choose a blouse and fix her eyebrows. Then, when he came, probably nothing would happen, but at least she'd have enjoyed the buildup. Besides, what did she have to lose? With anyone else, she'd be worrying about being let down, but with David there was nothing left to worry about. The guy had already let her down the last time they met, yapping away about how much he loved her and, after they made out a little and she gave him a hand job, falling asleep on his hotel bed. He hadn't called the next day, nor the day after that. And two days later, she'd stopped expecting him to. She knew he'd gone back to Cleveland, or Portland, or whatever his hometown in America was called. And it hurt. It hurt like when someone sees you on the street and pretends they don't recognize you. If she were to meet him on the street in Cleveland or Portland, or wherever, and he'd been there with his girlfriend, that's what would have happened for sure.

Back then, he told her about his girlfriend. And that they were going to get married. She couldn't claim he'd kept it from her. But there was something in the way he said it that made her feel like it had been true until the moment he met her and that now his life was taking a whole new direction, one that included her. But she must have gotten it wrong, or he must have given her the wrong impression. It all depends on how you look at it. And on the mood she was in when she pictured the two of them at the hotel. Sometimes she'd tell herself, Lay off, you moron. He's American, what did you expect? You think he'd dump his whole life over there—the job at the JCC that he tried to tell you about? That he'd come here to work as a barman or a delivery boy just to be with you? But other times, she'd get mad. Why did he have to use that word *love*? He could have just told her he was attracted to her or that he was horny, drunk, and far from home. Chances were she'd have given him a hand job anyway, but without hanging around at home for two days afterward, waiting for the phone to ring. She didn't have a cell phone back then, so she just sat around and waited. It was summer then too, and her apartment wasn't air-conditioned. The air in the room wasn't moving, and all day long she tried to read a book—*Underworld* by Don DeLillo—but by the end of the day she was still stuck at the Prologue. She couldn't remember a thing she'd read. Something about a baseball game. She never went back to it after that, and David never called. But now, almost a year later, suddenly he did, and when he asked if he could drop by, she said okay, mainly because she didn't want him to notice that a part of her had been hurt. She didn't want him to think he mattered so much that she wouldn't want to see him again.

He brought a bottle of wine and a pizza. Half olive, half anchovy. He didn't even phone to ask her what she wanted or if she was hungry at all. But the pizza was really good. The wine was white and warm, but they didn't have the patience to wait for it to chill, so they drank it with ice cubes. "A hundred-dollar bottle," he said, laughing, "and here we are, drinking it like Diet Coke." He must have wanted her to know he'd spent a lot of money on the wine. Since that night, he said, I've been feeling really lousy about what happened. I felt like shit. I should have phoned you the next morning to explain. In fact, I should have made sure it never happened in the first place. I'm sorry. And she patted his cheek, not seductively, but more like a mother comforting her son who's just owned up to cheating on an exam, and telling him it's not so terrible. Yes, she had thought about him. She'd wondered why he hadn't called. But in any case, he shouldn't feel bad about it. He'd told her from the start that he had a girlfriend and that was that.

They'd gotten married in the meantime, David told her. When he got back from Israel, Karen—that was her name— told him she was pregnant and they'd had to decide whether to have an abortion or stay together. When Karen talked to him about it, it was as soon as he got off the plane and he'd still had her scent in his hair. He hadn't showered since that night they were in bed together, so that the scent would linger. They'd have to decide whether to have an abortion or to stay together, Karen said. And he hadn't wanted to stay together. Because of her, because of that night. But he didn't want Karen to have an abortion either. It was hard for him to explain. He wasn't religious or anything. But the thought of an abortion seemed so irreversible and made him very uneasy. So he proposed. A baby is also irreversible, she told him now, as if it were a joke, and he cringed and said he knew that. And in the same breath, he added that it was a baby girl, and that it was the most wonderful thing that had ever happened to him. Even if he and Karen got divorced, he said, which he didn't think would happen, because they were doing okay on the whole, but even if it did happen, he was glad that Karen hadn't had an abortion. Their little girl was so incredibly adorable. On Friday she'd be five months old exactly, and this was the first time he'd been away since she was born. He'd almost decided not to come to this conference either. He must have changed his mind five times at least, but in the end he took the flight. Mainly to see her. To tell her he was sorry.

"I came here to ask you to forgive me," he said again. She wanted to tell him he was making too much of it. A mountain out of a molehill. But after another drawn-out silence, she said she forgave him. She'd never been in his situation, but she understood him completely. And she was just a little sorry that he'd never called. To say goodbye before he took off, that's all. "If I'd called," he said, "I would have come back. And if I'd come back, I would have fallen in love with you. I was scared." And if she'd wanted to make him feel bad, she could have mentioned that even back then, on that first night, he'd said he loved her, but instead, she just stroked his large hand as it rested on the table, and later they went into the living room together and watched an episode of *Lost* and finished off the wine. Three years ago, when Giora got her pregnant, she hadn't even asked him if he wanted her to have an abortion or wanted them to stay together. She just went ahead and had the abortion without telling him. Two months later, they split up. This David must have loved Karen a little more than she'd loved Giora. Or at least hated her less. She knew that this night could end wherever she wanted it to, and it made her feel strong. If she drew things out a bit till it got late and said she was tired, he would leave without trying anything. If she looked at him and smiled—he'd kiss her. She could tell. But what did she really want? For him to go back to his hotel room horny and masturbate and think about her, about how things had worked out okay? Or for him to spend the night with her and feel like shit the next day? She kept changing her mind. Forget about him, she told herself, forget about him and about how he'll feel. Think about yourself. What do you want?

Because of the cast, going to the bathroom was a whole production now. She had to hop on one leg and keep her balance. David wouldn't let her do this. He picked her up in his arms, like a fireman saving her from a burning building or a groom carrying her over the threshold on their wedding night. He waited behind the door as she peed, and then carried her back into the living room. By the time they got back, the episode was over. David told her the ending. He'd seen it already. In America, they screen it a week earlier. He hadn't told her before that he'd already seen it, because he didn't mind watching it again, with her. He wasn't much of a TV buff anyway. The first time, he'd watched it only because Karen was addicted to the series. It's hot in your apartment, he said. Stifling hot. She told him she knew. The owner had lowered the rent for her and her roommate by sixty bucks because there was no air conditioner. Since she'd broken her leg, she was stuck here, she said. At the hospital, they'd given her a pair of crutches, but who has the strength to walk down four flights of stairs on crutches? And before she realized what was happening, he lifted her onto his shoulders, piggyback, and they walked down the four flights. Just like that.

He carried her that way to Meyer Park, where they sat on a bench and smoked a cigarette. It was hot and humid there too, but at least there was a breeze to dry off the perspiration. Having you forgive me was really important to me, he said. Extremely important. I can't even explain why. It's not that I never behaved like shit before with girls I dated, but with you . . . he started crying. It took her a moment to realize this was what he was doing. At first she thought he was coughing or choking or something, but he was simply crying. Stop it, you jerk, she told him, half smiling. People are staring. They'll wind up thinking I threw you out, I broke your heart. I am a jerk, David told her, I really am. I could have . . . you've never been to Cleveland, have you? Talk about Cleveland and talk about Tel Aviv. She could tell he wanted to say, Talk about Karen and talk about you, and she was glad he didn't say it.

They walked back up the four flights of stairs very slowly. He couldn't carry her anymore, so she just leaned on him and hobbled up, step after step. By the time they reached the door, they were both sweating, and inside her cast, the maddening itch was starting up again. Do you want me to go, he asked, and she shook her head, but what she said was that she thought it would be a good idea. Afterward, in bed, facing the fan, she tried to make sense of the whole story. An American guy and an Israeli girl meet by sheer chance. One nice evening. A little spit on her left palm sliding up and down David's cock. And two people, on two sides of the ocean, wind up carrying around all these not-very-important details for almost a year. Some people fall out of the third floor of a building and end up with nothing more than a black-and-blue mark on their backside. While others take one wrong step on their way down the stairs and wind up with a cast. She and David were of the second kind.

WHAT DO WE HAVE IN OUR POCKETS?

A cigarette lighter, a cough drop, a postage stamp, a slightly bent cigarette, a toothpick, a handkerchief, a pen, two five-shekel coins. That's only a fraction of what I have in my pockets. So is it any wonder they bulge? Lots of people mention it. They say, "What the fuck do you have in your pockets?" Most of the time I don't answer, I just smile, sometimes I even give a short, polite laugh. As if someone told me a joke. If they were to persist and ask me again, I'd probably show them everything I have, I might even explain why I need all that stuff on me, always. But they don't. What the fuck, a smile, a short laugh, an awkward silence, and we're on to the next subject.

The fact is that everything I have in my pockets is carefully chosen so I'll always be prepared. Everything is there so I can be at an advantage at the moment of truth. Actually, that's not accurate. Everything's there so I won't be at a disadvantage at the moment of truth. Because what kind of advantage can a wooden toothpick or a postage stamp really give you? But if, for example, a beautiful girl—you know what, not even beautiful, just charming, an ordinary-looking girl with an entrancing smile that takes your breath away—asks you for a stamp, or doesn't even ask, just stands there on the street next to a red mailbox on a rainy night with a stampless envelope in her hand and wonders if you happen to know where there's an open post office at that hour, and then gives a little cough because she's cold, but also desperate, since deep in her heart she knows that there's no open post office in the area, definitely not at that hour, and at that moment, that moment of truth, she won't say, "What the fuck do you have in your pockets," but she'll be so grateful for the stamp, maybe not even grateful, she'll just smile that entrancing smile of hers, an entrancing smile for a postage stamp— I'd go for a deal like that anytime, even if the price of stamps soars and the price of smiles plummets.

After the smile, she'll say thank you and cough again, because of the cold, but also because she's a little embarrassed. And I'll offer her a cough drop. "What else do you have in your pockets?" she'll ask, but gently, without the *fuck* and without the negativity, and I'll answer without hesitation: Everything you'll ever need, my love. Everything you'll ever need.

So now you know. That's what I have in my pockets. A chance not to screw up. A slight chance. Not big, not even probable. I know that, I'm not stupid. A tiny chance, let's say, that when happiness comes along, I can say yes to it, and not "Sorry, I don't have a cigarette/toothpick/coin for the soda machine." That's what I have there, full and bulging, a tiny chance of saying yes and not being sorry.

BAD KARMA

"Fifteen shekels a month can guarantee your daughter one hundred thousand in the event of your death, God forbid. Do you know what a difference one hundred thousand can make to a young orphan? It's exactly the difference between life in a white-collar profession and life as a receptionist in a dentist's office."

Since the accident, Oshri had been selling policies like hot-cakes. It wasn't clear whether this had to do with his slight limp or with the paralysis in his right arm, but people who'd sit through an appointment with him would lap it all up, and buy everything he had to offer: life insurance, loss of earning power, complementary health insurance, you name it. At first Oshri kept recycling the one about the Yemenite who was run over by an ice-cream truck the very day he bought his policy, on his way to pick up his daughter from kindergarten, or the one about the guy from the suburbs who'd laughed when Oshri offered him health insurance and one month later called in tears, having just received a diagnosis of pancreatic cancer. But very soon he realized that his own personal story did the trick better than any of the others. There he was, Oshri Sivan, insurance agent, in the middle of a meeting with a potential client at a café near the Downtown Shopping Arcade, when all of a sudden, right in the middle of their conversation, a young man who'd decided to end his life jumps out of an eleventh-floor window in the building next to them, and wham! falls right on Oshri's head. The fall kills the young man, and Oshri, who has just finished telling his Yemenite-and-ice-cream-truck story to another reluctant client, loses consciousness on the spot. He doesn't come to when they splash water over his face, or in the ambulance, or in the emergency room, and not even in the ICU. He's in a coma. The doctors say it's touch and go. His wife sits at his bedside and cries and cries, and so does his little girl. Nothing changes for six weeks, until all of a sudden a miracle occurs: Oshri comes out of his coma, as if nothing had happened. He simply opens his eyes and gets up. And along with this miracle comes a bitter truth: our Oshri didn't practice what he preached, and since he'd never had any insurance whatsoever himself, he couldn't keep up with his mortgage and had to sell his apartment and move into a rental. "Look at me," Oshri would end his sad story, with a lame attempt to move his right arm. "Look at me, sitting here with you at this café, spitting blood to sell you a policy. If only I'd put aside thirty shekels a month— thirty shekels, which is nothing really, barely a matinee ticket without the popcorn—I'd be lying back like a king with two hundred grand in my account. Me, I had my chance and I blew it, but you—aren't you going to learn from my mistake, Motti? Sign on the dotted line and get it over with. Who knows what could land on your head five minutes from now." And this Motti or Yigal or Mickey sitting across from him would stare for a minute and then take the pen he held out with his good arm and sign. Every single one of them. No ifs, ands, or buts. And Oshri would wink goodbye, because when your right arm is paralyzed there's no shaking hands, and on his way out he'd be sure to add something about how they'd made the right move. And so, without much effort, Oshri Sivan's battered bank account quickly began to recover, and within three months he and his wife had bought a new apartment with a much smaller mortgage than the one they'd had before. And with all the physiotherapy he got at the clinic, even his arm started to get better, though when clients held out their hand to him, he'd still pretend he couldn't move it at all.

"There's blue and yellow and white and a soft sweet taste in my mouth. There's something hovering high above me. Something good, and I'm heading toward it. Heading toward it."

At night he went on dreaming about it—not about the accident. About the coma. It was strange, but even though a long time had passed since then, he could still remember, down to the last detail, everything he'd felt during those six weeks. He remembered the colors and the taste and the fresh air cooling his face. He remembered the absence of memory, the sense of existing without a name and without a history, in the present. Six whole weeks of present. During which the only thing he felt within him that wasn't the present was this little hint of a future, in the form of an unaccountable optimism attached to a strange sense of beingness. He didn't know what his own name was during those six weeks, or that he was married, or that he had a little girl. He didn't know he'd had an accident or that he was in the hospital now, fighting for his life. He didn't know anything except that he was alive. And this fact alone filled him with enormous happiness. All in all, the experience of thinking and feeling within that nothingness was more intense than anything that had ever happened to him before, as if all the background noises had disappeared and the only sound left was true and pure and beautiful to the point of tears. He didn't discuss it with his wife or with anyone else. You're not supposed to get that much joy out of being close to death. You're not supposed to get a thrill from your coma while your wife and daughter are crying their hearts out at your bedside. So when they asked whether he remembered anything about it, he said he didn't, he didn't remember a thing. When he woke up, his wife asked if, when he'd been in the coma, he'd been able to hear her and Meital, their daughter, talking to him, and he told her that even if he couldn't remember hearing them he was sure it had helped him. It had given him strength, on the unconscious level, and a desire to live. That was what he told her, but it wasn't true, because when he was in the coma he really did hear voices on the outside sometimes. Strange, sharp, yet at the same time unclear, like sounds you hear when you're underwater. And he didn't like it at all. Those voices sounded menacing to him, they hinted at something beyond the pleasant, colorful now in which he was living.

"May you never know sorrow again."

Oshri couldn't make it during the shiva week to pay a condolence call on the family of the guy who'd fallen on his head. He couldn't make it to the unveiling of the headstone either. But when the first anniversary rolled around, he did go, with flowers and everything. At the cemetery there were only the guy's parents and his sister and some fat high school friend. They didn't know who he was. The mother thought he was her son's boss, whose name was Oshri too. The sister and the fat guy thought he was a friend of the parents. But after everyone had finished placing little stones on the grave and the mother started asking around, he explained that he was the one that Nattie, that was the guy's name, had landed on when he jumped out the window. As soon as the mother heard this, she started saying how sorry she was, and couldn't stop crying. The father tried to calm her down, and kept giving Oshri suspicious looks. After five minutes of her hysterical sobbing, the father told Oshri stiffly how sorry he was for everything that had happened to him and that he was sure that Nattie, too, if he were still alive, would be sorry, but that now it would be better for everyone if Oshri left. Oshri agreed at once and quickly added that he was almost fine by now and that when all was said and done it hadn't been so terrible—certainly not when you compared it with what Nattie's parents had been through. The father cut him short in mid-sentence: "Are you planning to sue us? Because if you are, you're wasting your time. Ziva and I haven't got a penny to our names, you hear me? Not a penny." The words only made the mother cry harder, and Oshri mumbled something that was supposed to reassure them, about how he had no hard feelings against anyone, and after that, he left. As he was putting the cardboard yarmulke back in the wooden box at the entrance to the cemetery, Nattie's sister caught up with him and apologized for her father. She didn't exactly apologize, actually, just said that he was an idiot and that Nattie had always hated him. His father, it turned out, had always been sure everyone was out to get him, and in the end that was what really happened, when his partner ran off with his money. "If Nattie could see how things here turned out, he'd be laughing hysterically," the sister said, and she introduced herself by name. Her name was Maayan. Out of habit, Oshri didn't take the hand she held out to him. After a year of pretending with clients that his arm was utterly paralyzed, it had got to the point where even when he was home alone he sometimes forgot he could use it. When Maayan saw that he wasn't taking her outstretched hand, she shifted the handshake ever so naturally and touched him on the shoulder—which, it turned out, made both of them a little uneasy. "It's strange having you here," she said after they had both been silent for a moment. "What is Nattie to you? You didn't even know him, after all." "That's a shame," Oshri said, not sure how to respond. "That I didn't know him, I mean. He sounds like somebody who was definitely worth knowing." Oshri wanted to tell her that his coming there wasn't strange at all. That he and her brother had some unfinished business between them. There had been so many people at the café that day, and of all the people there, he was the one that Nattie had dropped on top of. And that was why he'd come today, to try to understand why. But even before he had a chance to say it, he realized it would sound stupid, so he asked her instead why Nattie had killed himself—so young and all. Maayan shrugged. He wasn't the first person to ask her that. Before they went their separate ways, he gave her his business card and said that if she needed any help, no matter what it was, she should call. And she smiled and thanked him but said she was someone who managed very well on her own. After taking another look at the card, she said, "You're an insurance agent? That's really strange. Nattie always hated insurance, said it was bad karma. That taking out a policy was like the opposite of believing things would go well." Oshri got defensive. Lots of young people think that way, he said, but once you have children you look at things differently. And even if you want to believe things will go well, you can never be too careful. "Still, if you need anything," he told her before she left, "do call. I promise not to try to sell you insurance." And she smiled and nodded. They both knew she wouldn't be calling.

While Oshri was on his way home from the cemetery, his wife phoned. She wanted him to pick up Meital from the class she took after school. Oshri agreed right away, and when she asked him where he was, he lied and said he'd had an appointment with a client in Ramat Hasharon. He couldn't explain to himself why he'd lied. It wasn't because of the touch he could still feel on his shoulder, and it wasn't because he'd gone to the memorial service for no good reason. If anything, it was because he was afraid she'd get a sense of how grateful he was to that guy, Nattie, who must have been just as smart, as successful, and as loved as Oshri was, and had still decided to put an end to it all and jump out the window. When he picked up Meital, she proudly showed him a model airplane she'd built, and he admired it and asked her when she was planning to fly it in the sky. "Never," Meital said, and gave him a derisive look. "It's just a model." And Oshri nodded, embarrassed, and said she was such a smart little girl.

PLEASANT DREAMS

Ever since the accident, he and his wife made love a lot less often. They never talked about it, but he had the feeling she thought it was okay too. As if after the accident and everything she was just so glad to have him back that she wasn't planning to keep score. Whenever they did make love it was nice, just as nice as it had been before, except that now his life had taken on another perspective, one that had to do with that world, a world you can reach only when something falls on you from the top floor, a perspective that seemed to have dwarfed everything else. Not just the sex, but his love for her too, and his love for his daughter, everything.

When he was awake he couldn't remember exactly what it had felt like to be in the world of the coma, and if he tried to describe it to someone, he couldn't. He tried only once, with this blind woman to whom he'd been trying to sell life insurance. He wasn't sure why he'd expected her, of all people, to understand, but after three sentences he realized he was only scaring her, so he stopped. In his dreams, though, he really could go back there. And ever since that day in the cemetery, his coma dreams recurred more often. He felt himself becoming addicted to them. So much so that in the evenings, long before he got into bed, he would begin to tremble in anticipation, like someone who after many years in exile was getting on the flight that would take him home. It's funny, but sometimes he was so excited that he couldn't even fall asleep. And then he'd find himself lying in bed, frozen, next to his sleeping wife, trying to lull himself to sleep in all sorts of ways. One of them was masturbation. And ever since that memorial service, whenever he masturbated, he'd think of Maayan, of how she'd touched him on his shoulder. It wasn't because she was beautiful. And it wasn't that she wasn't beautiful, though her beauty was the fragile kind that comes with youth, the kind whose expiration date was coming up very, very soon. As it happened, his wife had once had that same kind of beauty, many years ago, when they first met. But that wasn't the reason he would think of Maayan. It was because of the connection between her and the man who had helped him reach that world of colors and quiet, and when he'd masturbate over Maayan, it was as if he were masturbating over a world that suddenly, thanks to her, had taken on a woman's shape.

Meanwhile, he was churning out policies at a dizzying pace. Without even meaning to, he was getting better and better at it. Now, when he tried to sell them, he'd often find himself in tears. It wasn't a manipulation. It was real crying that came out of nowhere. And it would shorten the meetings. Oshri would cry and then he'd apologize, and right away the clients would say it was okay and sign. It made him feel a little like a swindler, the crying, though it was as genuine as could be.

CONGESTION ON THE COASTAL ROAD

One weekend when they were returning with their daughter from a visit to his wife's parents on a kibbutz, they passed a two-car collision. The drivers ahead of them slowed down to rubberneck, and his wife said it was disgusting, and that only in Israel did people behave that way. Their daughter, who'd been asleep in the back, woke up because of the ambulance sirens. She put her face up to the window and looked out at a man covered in blood, unconscious, being carried away on a stretcher. She asked them where they were taking him, and Oshri told her they were taking him to a good place. A place filled with colors and tastes and smells that you couldn't even imagine. He told her about that place, about how your body becomes weightless there, and how even though you don't want anything, everything there comes true. How there's no fear there, so that even if something is going to hurt, when it happens it turns into just another kind of feeling, a feeling that you're grateful to be able to have. He went on and on until he noticed the angry look on his wife's face. On the radio they reported heavy traffic on the highway, and when he looked in the rearview mirror again he could see Meital smiling and waving bye-bye at the man on the stretcher.

ARI

When she comes, my girlfriend screams out "Ari." Not just
once, a lot. "Ari-Ari-Ari-Ari!" And that's just fine, as I'm an
Ari born and raised. Still, sometimes I kind of want her to
yell something else, it wouldn't matter what. "My love." "Tear
me in half." "Stop, I can't take any more." Even a plain old
"Don't stop!" would do. It'd just be nice to hear something
different once in a while, something specific to the occa-
sion—an emotion a little more to the point.

My girlfriend is a law student at the local college. She
wanted to go to one of the big universities but they didn't
take her. Right now she's gearing up to specialize in contract
law. There's really a thing like that, lawyers who deal only
with contracts. They don't meet with people, they don't ap-
pear in court, they just sit there all day looking at line after
line printed on paper, as if that makes up a world.

She was there with me when I rented the apartment.
And within a minute she caught the owner trying to bam-
boozle us on some clause. In a million years I'd never have
noticed, but she spotted it in a flash. My girlfriend, she's box-
cutter sharp. And how she comes. In my life, I've never seen
anything like it. Her flying in every direction, body in full

riot. It's like seeing someone electrocuted. She gets swallowed up by these waves of convulsions, involuntary ones, from deep inside. They rumble their way into her neck and tickle the soles of her feet. It's like her whole anatomy is trying to say thanks without knowing how.

One time I asked her what she used to yell when she came with other guys—back before me. She stared at me, surprised, and said that with all of them, when she came, she yelled "Ari." Always "Ari." And I couldn't let it go. I asked her what she used to say when she came with guys that didn't happen to be named Ari. She thought about it for a minute, and said that she'd never once fucked anyone who wasn't named Ari. Twenty-eight guys she'd already bedded, including me, and all of them—now that she was thinking back on it—were Aris, every last one. After she said it, she went silent. And then, real calmly, I told her, "That's one crazy coincidence . . . or maybe that's your whole selection process, finding a new Ari." "Maybe so," she said, all thoughtful. "Maybe so."

From that moment on, I became hyperaware of all the Aris in my midst: there's the one at the falafel stand, and my accountant, and there's the pushy one at our coffee shop who's always asking me to put the sports section aside. I didn't make a big deal out of it, just made a mental note—Ari+Ari+Ari. Because deep down I knew, when all the torment is unleashed—*if* it's unleashed—it will spring from one of those guys.

It's strange to tell you so much about my girlfriend without even mentioning her name. As if it's of no importance at all. Except that it really isn't. If you woke me in the middle of the night, it's not her name that would come to mind. It would be that half-surprised look of hers one second before she starts to cry that would float through my head; or a vision of her ass; or that beautiful, childlike way she always says "I want to tell you something" right before sharing a thought that moves her. My girl, she's fantastic. But sometimes I'm not so sure that this whole story will end well.

Our landlord, the one that tried to fleece us with the lease, he's also named Ari. He's basically nothing but a fifty-year-old prick whose dead grandmother left him a whole building five blocks from the beach. Apart from collecting checks from his tenants, the man hasn't done a stroke of work in his life. He's also got the kind of blue eyes you see on fighter pilots, and silver-gray hair that shines like the god-damn edge of a cloud. But this guy's no pilot. When we signed the agreement, he told me that he passed his whole military service pushing papers at Tzrifin, on some transport base. It'd been maybe a dozen years since his reserve unit even bothered to check where he was.

It was only by happenstance that I discovered he was fucking her. If she hadn't let me in on this whole story of the Aris, I wouldn't have been suspicious. When I caught them both in the apartment, he was in the living room, fully dressed. He said he'd come by to check that we weren't "destroying his assets." Right after he left, I pressed her and she came out and admitted it. But this was a confession with no guilt attached to it: when she spoke, her tone was completely matter-of-fact, totally dry. She told me the way a stranger would tell you the number 8 bus doesn't stop at Dizengoff. And as soon as she's done, she says she has something to ask. What she wants to know is if we can all do it once, together. Him and me, both.

She's even willing to make a deal. If we do it just once,

she won't ever see him again. Just once in her life she wants to feel a pair of Aris inside her together. He'll definitely agree, bored perv that he is. She's sure of it. And in the end I'll also give in, because I love her. I genuinely do.

And that's how I find myself in bed with my landlord. One second before he strips down he's still haranguing me about the shutters in the kitchen, that they don't close right, that I need to oil up some hinge. After a while, my girlfriend's body starts to shake up above me. I sense she's on her way. And I can tell that when she screams, somehow, everything will be all right. Because our name is truly Ari. Only, what we'll never know is if her scream is him or if it is me.

BITCH

Widower. He loved the sound of that word so much, loved it, but at the same time was ashamed that he loved it, but what can you do, love is an uncontrollable emotion. *Bachelor* always sounded a bit egotistical to him, hedonistic, and *divorced*— defeated; even more, totaled. But *widower? Widower* sounds like someone who took responsibility, was committed, and if he was now on his own, you could only blame God or the forces of nature, depending on where you're coming from. He took out a cigarette and was about to light it when the anorexic girl sitting across from him in the car started grumbling in French and pointing to the sign NON FUMEUR. Who would've believed that on the Marseilles–Paris train they don't let a person light a Gauloise. Before he became a widower, every time he was about to light up, it was Bertha who broke into a monologue that began with his health and, somehow, always ended with her migraines, and now, when that too-skinny French girl yelled at him, he suddenly missed her.

"My wife," he said to the French girl as he showed her that he was putting the cigarette back in the pack, "also don't like me to smoke."

"No English," the French girl said.

"You," he persisted, "same age like my daughter. You should eat more. It is not healthy."

"No English," the French girl repeated, but her hunching shoulders gave her away: She understood every word.

"My daughter live in Marseilles," he continued. "She is married to a doctor, an eye doctor, you know." He pointed at one of her green eyes, which were blinking in fear.

Even the coffee on the train was on a level three times higher than anything you could find in Haifa. Yessir, when it came to taste, those damn French outclassed everyone. After a week in Marseilles, he couldn't button his pants. Zahava had wanted him to stay longer. "Where are you rushing off to?" she'd asked. "Now that Mom's dead and you're retired, you're all alone." *Alone* and *retired*, there was something so open about those two words that when she said them, he could feel the wind on his face. After all, he'd never really liked working in the store, and Bertha, well, he did have a soft spot for her, but, like the wooden wardrobe in their tiny bedroom, she took up so much space that there was no room left alongside her for anything else. The first thing he did after she died was call the junkman and get rid of that wardrobe. To the neighbors watching with interest as the huge wardrobe slid down from the third floor on belts, he explained that it reminded him too much of the tragedy. The tragedy. Now, without that wardrobe, the room had suddenly become spacious and lighter. After all those years, he'd forgotten a window was hidden behind it.

In the dining car, a woman of about seventy was sitting across from him. She'd been beautiful once, and she did everything she could to remind people of that. But she did it subtly, with artful touches of lipstick and eyeliner. "Ah . . . if you could only have seen me fifty years ago." Next to her, on the shelf meant for food trays, sat a small poodle, also dressed elegantly, in an embroidered, powder-blue sweater. The poodle fixed huge, familiar eyes on him. "Bertha?" he thought to himself, half-terrified. The poodle gave a short bark in confirmation. The old woman flashed a pleasant smile at him that tried to say he had nothing to be afraid of. The poodle's eyes never left his. "I know that wardrobe didn't fall on me by accident," they said. "I know you pushed it." He took a short drag on his cigarette and shot a nervous smile back at the woman. "And I know that you didn't want to kill me, that it was just a reflex. When I asked you to take down the winter clothes again, you just lost control." His head seemed to nod on its own—another reflex, apparently. If he'd been someone else, less tough, there would already have been tears in his eyes. "Are you happy now?" the poodle's eyes asked. "So-so." He looked back at it. "It's hard alone. And you?" "Not bad." The poodle opened its mouth into almost a smile. "My mistress takes care of me; she's a good woman. How's our daughter?" "I'm just coming from her place. She looks wonderful, and Gilbert finally agreed to try to have a baby." "I'm glad." The poodle wagged its stumpy tail. "But you, you have to take better care of yourself. You've gotten fat, and you smoke too much." "May I?" he asked the old woman without words, making petting motions in the air. The old woman nodded and smiled. He petted Bertha's whole body, then bent down and kissed her. "I'm sorry," he said in a broken, tearful voice. "I'm sorry, Bertha, forgive me." "She love you," the old woman said in broken English. "Look, look how she lick your face. I never see her like that with a stranger."

THE STORY, VICTORIOUS

This story is the best story in the book. More than that, this story is the best story in the world. And we weren't the ones to come to that conclusion. It was also reached by a unanimous team of dozens of unaffiliated experts who—employing strict laboratory standards—measured it against a representative sampling taken from world literature. This story is a unique Israeli innovation. And I bet you're asking yourselves, how is it that we (tiny little Israel) composed it, and not the Americans? What you should know is that the Americans are asking themselves the same thing. And more than a few of the bigwigs in American publishing stand to lose their jobs because they didn't have that answer at the ready while it still mattered.

Just as our army is the best army in the world—same with this story. We're talking here about an opening so innovative that it's protected by registered patent. And where is this patent registered? That's the thing, it's registered in the story itself! This story's got no shtick to it, no trick to it, no touchy-feely bits. It's forged from a single block, an amalgam of deep insights and aluminum. It won't rust, it won't bust, but it may wander. It's supercontemporary, and timelessly literary. Let History be the judge! And by the way, according to many fine folk, judgment's been passed—and our story came up aces.

"What's so special about this story?" people ask out of innocence or ignorance (depending on who's asking). "What's it got that isn't in Chekhov or Kafka or I-don't-know-who? The answer to that question is long and complicated. Longer than the story itself, but less complex. Because there's nothing more intricate than this story. Nevertheless, we attempt to answer by example. In contrast to works by Chekhov and Kafka, at the end of this story, one lucky winner—randomly selected from among all the correct readers—will receive a brand-new Mazda Lantis with a metallic gray finish. And from among the incorrect readers, one special someone will be selected to receive another car, cheaper, but no less impressive in its metallic grayness so that he or she shouldn't feel bad. Because this story isn't here to condescend. It's here so that you'll feel good. What's that saying printed on the place mats at the diner near your house? ENJOYED YOURSELF—TELL YOUR FRIENDS! DIDN'T ENJOY YOURSELF—TELL US! Or, in this case—report it to the story. Because this story doesn't just tell, it also listens. Its ears, as they say, are attuned to every stirring of the public's heart. And when the public has had enough and calls for someone to put an end to it, this story won't drag its feet or grab hold of the edges of the altar. It will, simply, stop.

THE STORY, VICTORIOUS II

But if one day, out of nostalgia, you suddenly want the story back, it will always be happy to oblige.

A GOOD ONE

SO REAL

The night before his flight to New York, Gershon's wife had a dream. "It was so real," she told him as he packed. "The curbs were red and white and the electric poles had those apartments-for-sale ads posted on them—you know? The kind with those tabs you can pull off, just like in real life. There was even a man scooping his dog's shit off the sidewalk with a piece of newspaper. It was all so *ordinary*, so everyday." Gershon was attempting to cram more and more clothing and brochures into his small suitcase. His wife usually helped him pack, but this morning she was so engrossed in this so-real, so-detailed dream of hers that helping hadn't even occurred to her. The dream itself probably hadn't lasted more than ten seconds in the real world, but the way she managed to drag it out was making Gershon so angry that he was on the verge of tears. In three hours' time he'd be on a plane to New York, on his way to meet the largest toy manufacturer in the world, and when we say *largest in the world*, that's not just another tired cliché, but a fact based on a large number of balance sheets and sales figures, and if Gershon played his cards right, that manufacturer might buy the Stop—Police board game Gershon had developed and turn it into no less than the twenty-first-century Monopoly. And while none of that is exactly a red-and-white curb or a piece of dog shit being picked up with a wrinkled financial supplement, the idea that such monumental success might be on the horizon is the kind of thing you'd like to see your wife react to with a little more enthusiasm. " . . . And then my dad suddenly appears right in front of me with a baby carriage and says to me, 'Watch her.' Just like that. Leaves the carriage next to me and walks off like it's the most natural thing in the world," his wife continued as Gershon tried unsuccessfully to zip up his suitcase. "And the baby girl in the carriage looked so sad and alone, like an old woman, that I just wanted to take her in my arms and hug her. And it was all so real that when I woke up it took me a minute to figure out how I'd gone from the middle of the street to our bedroom. You know that feeling?"

RESTLESS

The albino sitting next to him tried to start a conversation. Gershon answered politely but didn't open up. He'd flown enough times to know the dynamic. There are some people who are just open and pleasant, and there are others who try to develop a little intimacy with you just so that, after take-off, when they take over the armrest you share, you'll feel embarrassed enough to let them have it. "My first time in America," the albino said. "I've heard that the police there are completely crazy. They'll throw you in jail just for jay-walking." "It'll be fine," Gershon answered curtly, and closed his eyes. He pictured himself entering the office of the Global Toys CEO, giving the silver-haired man standing in front of him a warm, firm handshake, and saying, "You have grandkids, Mr. Lipskar? Let me tell you what they'll be playing this summer." His left leg kept banging against the side of the plane. He had to remember not to jiggle his legs during the meeting, he told himself, it projects a lack of confidence.

He didn't touch the meal they served on the plane. The albino devoured the chicken and the salad as if they were gourmet food. Gershon glanced at his tray again. It all looked bad. The cellophane-wrapped chocolate cake reminded him of the dog shit in his wife's dream. But the apple looked relatively okay. He wrapped it in a napkin and put it in his completely empty attaché case. I should have put a few brochures in there, he thought, what if my suitcase doesn't arrive?

WE'RE ALL HUMAN

It didn't. All the passengers, including the albino, had already gone. The empty luggage carousel revolved for another few minutes, then got tired and stopped. A Continental ground-service employee said that she was very sorry and wrote down his hotel address. "It's very rare," she said, "but mistakes do happen. We're all human, you know." Maybe. Even though there were moments when Gershon felt he wasn't. For instance, when Eran died in his arms in Laniado Hospital. If Gershon had been human, he probably would have cried or collapsed. People close to him told him that he just hadn't taken it in yet, he needed time; that it wouldn't hit him till he understood it with his heart, not just his brain. But ten years had passed since then and nothing had hit him. In the army, when they wouldn't let him go into officer training, he'd cried like a girl. He remembered how the company's sergeant major had stared at him in helpless shock, but when his best friend died, nothing.

"We will of course compensate you with one hundred and twenty dollars against a bill for clothes and personal items," the ground employee said.

"Personal items," Gershon repeated.

She took the repetition as a question. "You know, a toothbrush, shaving cream. It's all spelled out on the back of the form." She pointed to the right place on the page and added, "I am really and truly sorry."

A GOOD ONE

Standing in the lobby of the Global Toys building was a young guy in a cheap suit. A pencil mustache rested not quite naturally above his open mouth, as if his upper lip were embarrassed about something and had decided to wear a toupee. Gershon wanted to ask him where the elevator was but, a second later, spotted it himself. He knew that Mr. Lipskar would consider him unprofessional because he had no brochures. He should have thought about that in advance and at least packed the presentation in his carry-on luggage. He probably would have if that annoying dream of his wife's hadn't been bouncing around in the space of his skull while he was packing. "I.D., please," Mustache said, and Gershon replied, surprised, "Excuse me?" "An I.D.," Mustache repeated, and said to the bald black guy in the gray jacket standing next to him, "You see the kind of characters we get here?"

Gershon went through his pockets slowly. In Israel he

was used to always showing identification, but this was the first time someone outside the country had asked him for anything like that, and somehow, Mustache's tough New York accent made it sound as if, in another second, he'd cuff him and read him his rights. "They take their time, don't they?" Mustache said to the black guy in the jacket. "Why not?" Jacket smiled a soft, yellow smile. "We're here anyway." "What can I tell you, Patrick," Mustache said, glancing at the passport Gershon handed him, "your mother didn't name you Patrick for nothing. You're a saint." He handed the passport back to Gershon and mumbled something. Gershon nodded and started walking toward the elevator. "Hold on," Mustache said, "where are you running to? Hey, you, don't you understand English?" "Actually, I do understand English," Gershon answered impatiently, "and if you don't mind, I'm in a hurry to get to a meeting." "I asked you to open your briefcase, Mr. Actually-I-Do-Understand-English," Mustache said, imitating Gershon's Israeli accent. "Will you do that for me?" And he said to Jacket, who was standing next to him, having the time of his life, trying not to smile, "I'm telling you, it's a zoo in here." Gershon thought about the half-eaten apple in his empty attaché case. He tried to imagine Mustache's wiseass reaction when he saw it, and Jacket next to him losing the battle to control himself and bursting out laughing. "Well, open it already," Mustache continued. "You know what *open* means, sir?" And he quickly spelled the word. "I know what *open* means," Gershon replied, clutching the attaché case to his chest with both hands. "I also know what *closed* means, and *nominal yield*, and *oxymoron*. I even know the second law of thermodynamics and what Wittgenstein's tractatus is. I know lots of things you'll never know, you arrogant little nothing.

And one of those amazing secrets you'll never get to host under the very thin skin of your brain is what I have in my attaché case. Do you even know who I am? Why I came here today? Do you even know anything about existence? The world? Anything beyond the number of the bus that takes you here and home every day, beyond the names of the neighbors in that dark, crummy building you live in? "Sir . . ." Jacket tried to stop the flow with pragmatic politeness, but it was too late. "I look at you," Gershon went on, "and in a second I see your whole life story. Everything's written right there, on that receding hairline of yours. Everything. The best day of your life will be when the basketball team you root for wins the championship. The worst day will be when your fat wife dies of cancer because your medical insurance doesn't cover the treatment. And everything that comes between those two moments will pass like a weak fart so that at the end of your life, when you try to look back, you won't even be able to remember what it smells like . . ."

Gershon didn't even have time to feel the fist connect with his face. When he came to, he found himself on the lobby's elegant marble floor. What revived him was a series of kicks to the ribs and a deep, pleasant voice echoing in the space of the lobby that reminded him a little of a late-night radio announcer's voice. "Let it go," the voice repeated, "let it go, Jesus, he's not worth it."

He noticed now that embedded in the floor were small gold stones forming the letter G—the first letter of his first name. He could have chalked it up to coincidence, but Gershon chose to imagine that the construction workers who built this skyscraper knew that he'd come here one day and wanted to make some kind of gesture in his honor so he wouldn't feel so alone and unwanted in this evil city. The kicks didn't stop and they felt so real, just like his wife's dream. Maybe the baby girl her father left in the carriage was actually her. Could be. After all, her father was kind of a shit. Maybe that's why the dream was so important to her. And if she'd needed a hug in the dream, he could have hugged her. He could have taken a second's break from his fucking struggle with the traitorous suitcase, which at this very moment was probably sniffing strangers' ankles on a carousel in some tiny airport on the West Coast, hold her tightly in his arms, and tell her, "I'm here, sweetheart, I may be flying today but I'll be back soon."

The black guy in the gray jacket helped him up. "You okay, sir?" he asked, and he handed him his attaché case and a tissue. "You're bleeding a little." He said *a little* in a gentle, muted voice, as if he were trying to shrink it to the size of a drop. Mustache was sitting on a chair near the elevator, crying. "I apologize for him," Jacket said, "he's going through a tough time right now." The word *tough* he enlarged. Almost shouted. "Don't apologize," Mustache said through his tears, "don't say you're sorry to that bastard." Jacket began shrugging and sniffling helplessly. "His mother . . ." he tried to whisper to Gershon. "Don't tell him," Mustache wept, "don't you say a word about my mother, you hear? Or I'll let you have a good one too."

RORSCHACH

"Stop—Police," Gershon went on, "might be the first board game in history that doesn't impose solutions on the child playing it but stimulates him to find his own solutions. You can think of the game as a sort of path of Rorschach blots that encourage you to use your imagination as you progress toward your goal—to win." "A path of Rorschach blots." Mr. Lipskar gave a crooked smile. "Amazing. I like it, Mr. Arazi. But are you sure you're really all right?" "I'm fine." Gershon nodded. "With your permission, could we perform a small simulation of the game now?" "Simulation," Mr. Lipskar repeated. He was a lot younger than Gershon had imagined, not a trace of gray in his shiny black hair. "I'm sorry, but I don't think this is the right time for that. Your eye. And your nose. My God, so much blood! Who did this to you?"

WHAT, OF THIS GOLDFISH, WOULD YOU WISH?

Yonatan had a brilliant idea for a documentary. He'd knock on doors. Just him. No camera crew, no nonsense. Just Yonatan, on his own, a small camera in hand, asking, "If you found a talking goldfish that granted you three wishes, what would you wish for?"

Folks would give their answers, and Yoni would edit them down and make clips of the more surprising responses. Before every set of answers, you'd see the person standing stock-still in the entrance to his house. Onto this shot he'd superimpose the subject's name, family situation, monthly income, and maybe even the party he'd voted for in the last election. All that, combined with the three wishes, and maybe he'd end up with a poignant piece of social commentary, a testament to the massive rift between our dreams and the often compromised reality in which we live.

It was genius, Yoni was sure. And, if not, at least it was cheap. All he needed was a door to knock on and a heart beating on the other side. With a little decent footage, he was sure he'd be able to sell it to Channel 8 or Discovery in a flash, either as a film or as a bunch of vignettes, little cinematic corners, each with that singular soul standing in a doorway, followed by three killer wishes, precious, every one.

Even better, maybe he'd cash out, package it with a slogan and sell it to a bank or cellular phone company. Maybe tag it with something like "Different dreams, different wishes, one bank." Or "The bank that makes dreams come true."

No prep, no plotting, natural as can be, Yoni grabbed his camera and went out knocking on doors. In the first neighborhood he went to, the kindly folk that took part generally requested the foreseeable things: health, money, bigger apartments, either to shave off a couple of years or a couple of pounds. But there were also powerful moments. One drawn, wizened old lady asked simply for a child. A Holocaust survivor with a number on his arm asked very slowly, in a quiet voice—as if he'd been waiting for Yoni to come, as if it weren't an exercise at all—he'd been wondering (if this fish didn't mind), would it be possible for all the Nazis left living in the world to be held accountable for their crimes? A cocky, broad-shouldered lady-killer put out his cigarette and, as if the camera wasn't there, wished he were a girl. "Just for a night," he added, holding a single finger right up to the lens.

And these were wishes from just one short block in one small, sleepy suburb of Tel Aviv. Yonatan could hardly imagine what people were dreaming of in the development towns and the collectives along the northern border, in the West Bank settlements and Arab villages, the immigrant absorption centers full of broken trailers and tired people left to broil out in the desert sun.

Yonatan knew that if the project was going to have any weight, he'd have to get to everyone, to the unemployed, to the ultrareligious, to the Arabs and Ethiopians and American expats. He began to plan a shooting schedule for the coming days: Jaffa, Dimona, Ashdod, Sderot, Taibe, Talpiot.

Maybe Hebron, even. If he could sneak past the wall, Hebron would be great. Maybe somewhere in that city some beleaguered Arab man would stand in his doorway and, looking through Yonatan and his camera, looking out into nothingness, just pause for a minute, nod his head, and wish for peace—that would be something to see.

Sergei Goralick doesn't much like strangers banging on his door. Especially when those strangers are asking him questions. In Russia, when Sergei was young, it happened plenty. The KGB felt right at home knocking on his door. His father had been a Zionist, which was pretty much an invitation for them to drop by any old time.

When Sergei got to Israel and then moved to Jaffa, his family couldn't wrap their heads around it. They'd ask him, "What are you looking to find in a place like that? There's no one there but addicts and Arabs and pensioners." But what is most excellent about addicts and Arabs and pensioners is that they don't come around knocking on Sergei's door. That way Sergei can get his sleep, and get up when it's still dark. He can take his little boat out into the sea and fish until he's done fishing. By himself. In silence. The way it should be. The way it was.

Until one day some kid with a ring in his ear, looking a little bit homosexual, comes knocking. Hard like that—rapping at his door. Just the way Sergei doesn't like. And he says, this kid, that he has some questions he wants to put on the TV.

Sergei tells the boy, tells him in what he thinks is a straightforward manner, that he doesn't want it. Not interested. Sergei gives the camera a shove, to help make it clear. But the earring boy is stubborn. He says all kinds of things, fast things. And it's hard for Sergei to follow; his Hebrew isn't so good.

The boy slows down, tells Sergei he has a strong face, a nice face, and that he simply has to have him for this movie picture. Sergei can also slow down, he can also make clear. He tells the kid to fuck off. But the kid is slippery, and somehow between saying no and pushing the door closed, Sergei finds that the kid is in his house. He's already making his movie, running his camera without any permission, and from behind the camera he's still telling Sergei about his face, that it's full of feeling, that it's tender. Suddenly the kid spots Sergei's goldfish flitting around in its big glass jar in his kitchen.

The kid with the earring starts screaming, "Goldfish, goldfish!" he's so excited. And this, this really pressures Sergei, who tells the kid, "It's nothing, just a regular goldfish, stop filming it. Just a goldfish," Sergei tells him, just something he found flapping around in the net, a deep-sea goldfish. But the boy isn't listening. He's still filming and getting closer and saying something about talking and fish and a magic wish.

Sergei doesn't like this, doesn't like that the boy is almost at it, already reaching for the jar. In this instant Sergei understands the boy didn't come for television, what he came for, specifically, is to snatch Sergei's fish, to steal it away. Before the mind of Sergei Goralick really understands what it is his body has done, he seems to have taken the burner off the stove and hit the boy in the head. The boy falls. The camera falls with him. The camera breaks open on the floor, along with the boy's skull. There's a lot of blood coming out of the head, and Sergei really doesn't know what to do.

That is, he knows exactly what to do, but it really would complicate things. Because if he takes this kid to the hospital, people are going to ask what happened, and it would take things in a direction Sergei doesn't want to go.

"No reason to take him to the hospital anyway," says the goldfish, in Russian. "That one's already dead."

"He can't be dead," Sergei says, with a moan. "I barely touched him. It's only a burner. Only a little thing." Sergei holds it up to the fish, taps it against his own skull to prove it. "It's not even that hard."

"Maybe not," says the fish. "But, apparently, it's harder than that kid's head."

"He wanted to take you from me," Sergei says, almost crying.

"Nonsense," the fish says. "He was only here to make a little something for TV."

"But he said—"

"He said," says the fish, interrupting, "exactly what he was doing. But you didn't get it. Honestly, your Hebrew, it's terrible."

"Yours is better?" Sergei says. "Yours is so great?"

"Yes. Mine's supergreat," the goldfish says, sounding impatient. "I'm a magic fish. I'm fluent in everything." All the while the puddle of blood from the earring kid's head is getting bigger and bigger and Sergei is on his toes, up against the kitchen wall, desperate not to step in it, not to get blood on his feet.

"You do have one wish left," the fish reminds Sergei. He says it easy like that, as if Sergei doesn't know—as if either of them ever loses count.

"No," Sergei says. He's shaking his head from side to side. "I can't," he says. "I've been saving it. Saving it for something."

"For what?" the fish says.

But Sergei won't answer.

That first wish, Sergei used up when they discovered a

cancer in his sister. A lung cancer, the kind you don't get better from. The fish undid it in an instant—the words barely out of Sergei's mouth. The second wish Sergei used up five years ago, on Sveta's boy. The kid was still small then, barely three, but the doctors already knew something in her son's head wasn't right. He was going to grow big but not in the brain. Three was about as smart as he'd get. Sveta cried to Sergei in bed all night. Sergei walked home along the beach when the sun came up, and he called to the fish, asked the goldfish to fix it as soon as he'd crossed through the door. He never told Sveta. And a few months later she left him for some cop, a Moroccan with a shiny Honda. In his heart, Sergei kept telling himself it wasn't for Sveta that he'd done it, that he'd wished his wish purely for the boy. In his mind, he was less sure, and all kinds of thoughts about other things he could have done with that wish continued to gnaw at him, half driving him mad. The third wish, Sergei hadn't yet wished for.

"I can restore him," says the goldfish. "I can bring him back to life."

"No one's asking," Sergei says.

"I can bring him back to the moment before," the goldfish says. "To before he knocks on your door. I can put him back to right there. I can do it. All you need to do is ask."

"To wish my wish," Sergei says. "My last."

The fish swishes his fish tail back and forth in the water, the way he does, Sergei knows, when he's truly excited. The goldfish can already taste freedom. Sergei can see it on him.

After the last wish, Sergei won't have a choice. He'll have to let the goldfish go. His magic goldfish. His friend.

"Fixable," Sergei says. "I'll just mop up the blood. A good sponge and it'll be like it never was."

That tail just goes back and forth, the fish's head steady.

Sergei takes a deep breath. He steps out into the middle of the kitchen, out into the puddle. "When I'm fishing, while it's dark and the world's asleep," he says, half to himself and half to the fish, "I'll tie the kid to a rock and dump him in the sea. Not a chance, not in a million years, will anyone ever find him."

"You killed him, Sergei," the goldfish says. "You murdered someone—but you're not a murderer." The goldfish stops swishing his tail. "If, on this, you won't waste a wish, then tell me, Sergei, what is it good for?"

It was in Bethlehem, actually, that Yonatan found his Arab, a handsome man who used his first wish for peace. His name was Munir; he was fat with a big white mustache. Superphotogenic. It was moving, the way he said it. Perfect, the way in which Munir wished his wish. Yoni knew even as he was filming that this guy would be his promo for sure.

Either him or that Russian. The one with the faded tattoos that Yoni had met in Jaffa. The one that looked straight into the camera and said, if he ever found a talking goldfish, he wouldn't ask of it a single thing. He'd just stick it on a shelf in a big glass jar and talk to him all day, it didn't matter about what. Maybe sports, maybe politics, whatever a goldfish was interested in chatting about.

Anything, the Russian said, not to be alone.

NOT COMPLETELY ALONE

Three of the guys she dated tried to commit suicide. She said that sadly but with a little bit of pride too. One of them even succeeded, jumped off the roof of the university humanities building and smashed his insides into thousands of pieces. On the outside he looked whole, even serene. She didn't get to the university that day but friends told her. Sometimes, when she's home alone, she can actually feel him there in the living room with her, looking at her, and when that happens, it's scary for a minute, but it makes her happy too. Because she knows she's not completely alone. As for me, she really likes me. Likes but isn't attracted. And that makes her sad, as sad as it makes me, maybe even more. Because she'd really like to be attracted to someone like me. Someone smart, someone gentle, someone who really loves her. She's been having an affair for a year with an older art dealer. He's married, doesn't plan to leave his wife, it's not even an option. He's someone she's actually attracted to. It's cruel. Cruel for me and cruel for her. Life would be much simpler is she were attracted to me.

She lets me touch her. Sometimes, when her back hurts, she even asks me to. When I massage her muscles she closes her eyes and smiles. "That feels good," she says, "really good."

Once we even had sex. In retrospect, it was a mistake, she says. Some part of her wanted so much for it to work that she ignored her senses. My smell, my body, something between us, just didn't click. She's been a psych major for four years now and she still can't explain it. How her mind wants to so much but her body just won't go along with it. Thinking about that night we went to bed together makes her sad. Lots of things make her sad. She's an only child. She spent a large part of her childhood alone. Her dad got sick, then was dying, then died. There was no brother to understand her, to console her. I'm the closest thing she has to a brother. Me and Kuti, that's the name of the guy who jumped off the roof of Humanities. She can sit and talk to me for hours about anything. She can sleep in the same bed with me, see me naked, be naked around me. Nothing between us embarrasses her. Not even when I masturbate next to her. Even though it stains the sheets and makes her sad. Makes her sad that she can't love me, but if it takes the edge off it for me, then she has no problem washing out the stains.

She and her dad were close before he died. She and Kuti were close too: He was in love with her. I'm the only guy close to her who's still alive. In the end, I'll start going out with another girl and she'll remain alone. It's bound to happen, she knows. And when it does, she'll be sad. Sad for herself, but also happy for me, that I found love. After I come, she strokes my face and says that even though it's sad, it's also flattering to her. Flattering that of all the girls in the world, she's the only one I think about when I masturbate. That art dealer she's sleeping with, he's hairy and shorter than me, but is he ever sexy. He served under Netanyahu in the army, and they've been in touch ever since. Real friends. Sometimes, when the art dealer comes to see her, he tells his wife he's go-ing to Bibi's. Once she bumped into him and his wife in the mall. They were standing a few feet away from each other; she gave him a small, secret smile and he ignored her. His eyes were on her but they were completely blank, as if she were nothing. As if she were empty air. And she understood that he couldn't smile back with his wife standing right there, or say anything to her, but even so, there was something very hurtful about it. She stood there by herself next to the pay phones and started to cry. That was the same night she slept with me. In retrospect, it was a mistake.

Four of the guys she dated tried to commit suicide. Two even succeeded. And they were the ones she cared about most. They were close to her, very close, like real brothers. Some-times when she's home alone she can actually feel us, Kuti and me, in the living room with her, looking at her. And when that happens, it's scary but it makes her happy too. Because she knows she's not completely alone.

ONE STEP BEYOND

Killers for hire, they're like wildflowers. They pop up in more species than you can name. I used to know one who called himself Maximillian Sherman, though I'm sure he had other aliases too. Max was one of those top-tier, high-end sorts of killers. Classy. The type that seals a deal maybe once or twice a year. And with the price he got per scalp, he didn't need to sign on for more.

My man Maximillian had gone vegetarian at the age of fourteen. He told me it was for reasons of conscience. He'd also adopted a kid from Darfur—a boy called Nuri. Max never once met the kid, but he'd write him long letters, and then Nuri would write him back and shove some photos in the envelope for good measure. What I'm trying to say is, Maximillian was a compassionate killer. He wouldn't murder children. Also, he had a problem with old ladies. That kind of high-mindedness cost him a lot of money over the course of his career. A whole lot of money.

So there's Maximillian, and then there's me. And that's what's lovely about this world of ours, that it's such a rich tapestry. I don't sound all polished like Maximillian. And you won't ever catch me with my nose buried in some scientific paper about toxins that can't be traced in the blood. But, in contrast to Mr. Sherman, I *am* willing to butcher an old lady. I'll kill children by the pound. And I'll do it without stuttering or blinking, and at no extra charge.

My lawyer says that's exactly why they stuck me with the death penalty. Today, he says, it's not like it used to be. In the old days folks preferred a public hanging over a good meal. These days people have lost their taste for killing murderers. It makes them sick to their stomachs, makes them feel bad about themselves. But child-killers? Those they still go after with gusto. Maybe you can make sense of it. As far as I can tell, a life is a life. And Maximillian Sherman and my righteous jurors can twist up their faces until the cows come home, but taking the life of a bulimic twenty-six-year-old student majoring in gender studies, or a sixty-eight-year-old limousine driver who fancies a bit of poetry on the side, that's no more or less all right than snuffing out the life of a runny-nosed three-year-old. Prosecutors love to split hairs over this. They love to mess with your head, talking about purity and helplessness. But a life is a life. And as a guy who's stood over plenty of corrupt lawyers and dirty politicians in his day, I've got to stress that at the appointed moment, the instant that the body gives a flutter and the eyes flip in their holes—right then, everyone is innocent and everyone helpless, not a lick of difference. But go and explain that to some half-deaf retired jurist from Miami whose experience of loss—apart from a husband she couldn't much stand—was nursing a pet hamster named Charlie as he succumbed to a case of cancer in his tiny-tiny colon.

In court they alleged that I am a hater of children. Maybe there's something to that. They dug up an old incident wherein I murdered a set of twins that weren't in the contract. It wasn't pro bono or anything, they just got caught up in the mix. And it's not that I've got any problem with kids when it comes to, say, their outward appearance. Because kids—in appearance—are actually pretty sweet. Like people, but small. They remind me of those mini cans of soda and eensy-weensy boxes of cereal that they used to hand out on planes. But behaviorwise? I'm sorry. I'm not exactly a fan of their little tantrums and breakdowns, the hysterics on the floor in the middle of the shopping mall. All that screeching, with the Daddy-should-go and I-don't-love-Mommy—and all because of some shitty two-dollar toy that, even if you buy it for them, won't get played with for more than a minute. I even hate the whole bedtime-story bit. It's not just the awkward situation where you're forced to lie next to them in their little uncomfortable beds, or that emotional blackmail of theirs. And, trust me, they don't hold back, they'll roll you over a barrel to get another story out of you; but, for me, the worst part is the stories themselves. Always precious, with sweet woodsy creatures stripped of their fangs and claws; illustrated lies about worlds without evil, places more boring than death. And if we're back on the subject of death: my lawyer thinks we can appeal the sentence. Not that it'll help. But making sure this whole performance reaches a higher court would buy us some time. I told him I'm not interested. Between us, what would I get from that little slice of living? More push-ups in a six-by-nine cell? More college basketball and crappy reality TV? If the only thing I've got coming down the pipeline is a needle full of poison, let them stick me now and move on. Let's not drag our feet.

When I was a kid, my father was always yammering on about heaven. He talked about it so much that he completely

lost sight of who, in this world, my mother was fucking behind his back. If my father's take on the world to come is
right, then it'll be anything but boring to be there. He was
Jewish, my father. But in prison, when they ask me, I request
a priest. Somehow, those Christians just seem a little less ab-
stract to me. And in my situation, the philosophical angle isn't
exactly relevant. What's important right now is the practical.
That I'll end up in hell is a given, and the more information
I manage to draw out of the priest, the better prepared I'll be
when I get there. I'm speaking from experience when I tell
you there's no place where crushing a kneecap or caving in a
skull won't increase your social standing. It doesn't matter if
it's a reform school in Georgia, basic training in the Marines,
or a closed prison wing in Bangkok. The wisdom is in being
able to identify on who, exactly, to crush what. And this is
precisely where the priest was supposed to help. In retrospect,
I see I could've requested a rabbi or a qadi or even a mute
Hindu baba, because that chatterbox priest hasn't helped at
all. He looks exactly like a Japanese tourist and must know it,
because the first thing he rushes to tell me is that he's already
a fourth-generation American, which is more than you can
say for me. The priest says that hell is completely personal.
Exactly like heaven. And in the end, everyone gets the hell
or the heaven he deserves. Still, I won't give up. Who's in
charge there? I ask him. How does it work? Is there any history of people that manage to escape? But he won't answer,
just nods his head up and down like those dogs you stick on
the dashboard. By the third time he asks me to take confession, I can't stand it anymore and I pop him real good. My
hands and my legs are restrained when I do it, so I've got to
use my head. The noggin is more than enough. I don't know

what materials they use to build Japanese priests nowadays, but mine came apart in an instant.

The guards that separate us beat me something serious: kicking, and clubbing, landing punches to the head. They act as if they're trying to subdue me, but they're just beating me silly for the hell of it. I understand them. It's fun to hit. The truth? I enjoyed that head butt to the priest more than the steak and fries they gave me for my last meal, and that prison steak wasn't half-bad. It's great fun to hit—and I can only imagine what violence awaits me on the far side of my shot of poison. I promise you that as much as it will be unpleasant for me in hell, it'll be worse for the son of a bitch standing within reach. And it won't matter to me if the guy's a run-of-the-mill sinner, or a demon, or Satan himself. That bleeding Japanese priest got my appetite going.

The needle hurts. They definitely could've found one that didn't, those self-righteous puritans, but they chose one with sting. They do it to punish.

While I'm dying, I remember everyone I killed. I see the expressions that spread over their faces right before their souls escaped through their ears. It's possible that they'll all be waiting there, seething, on the other side. Right then I feel one final, massive spasm take over my body, like someone's just closed a fist tight around my heart. My victims? Let them wait for me. I hope they're there! It'll be a pleasure to kill them all again.

I open my eyes. There's high green grass around me, like in the jungle. Somehow I imagined a hell more basement-like, all dark and dungeony. But here everything's green and the sun is high in the sky and dazzling. I forge a path forward, searching the ground for something I can use as a weapon: a stick, a stone, a sharpened branch. There's nothing. Nothing around me but tall grass and damp ground. That's when I notice a pair of giant human legs nearby. Whoever he is, he's eight times my size—and with me completely unarmed. I'll need to find his weak spots: knee, nuts, windpipe. I'll need to hit hard and hit fast and pray that it works. That's when the giant bends down. He's more agile than I expected. He plucks me into the air with force, and his mouth opens. Here you are, he says, and he holds me against his chest. Here you are, my sweet little bear. You know I love you more than anything in the world! I try to take advantage of our proximity, try to bite him on the neck, to shove a finger in his eye. I want to, but my body doesn't listen. It moves against my wishes, and there I am, hugging him back. Then it's the lips moving, beyond my control. They part and they whisper, I love you too, Christopher Robin. I love you more than anyone in the world.

BIG BLUE BUS

Some children throw themselves on the floor and have a tantrum. They cry and flail their arms and squirm till their faces turn red and sweaty and the saliva and mucus that drip out of their mouths and their noses start to stain the gray asphalt of the sidewalk. Be grateful he's not one of those.

Gilad clung to that thought in an attempt to calm himself. That thought and slow breathing. And it helped. On the sidewalk beside him was little Hillel, his fists clenched, his forehead wrinkled, his eyes shut tight, and his mouth whispering over and over again the same words, like a mantra: "I want to I want to I want to."

Gilad decides to smile before he starts talking. He knows Hillel can't actually see the smile, but hopes that, somehow, something of the smile will carry over in his voice. "Hillel, my sweet," he says through the smile, "Hillel, my precious, let's start walking before it's too late. They're having pancakes for breakfast in kindergarten today and unless we get there on time the other children will finish everything and won't leave you any."

I want to I want to I want to I want to I want to I want to I want to I want to I want to I want to I want to I want to I want to I want to I want to I want to I want to

Before he and Naama split up they had a rule about Hillel not watching television. Naama was the one who started it. She'd read something in *Haaretz*, and Gilad followed through with it. It seemed to make sense. But after they split up, they weren't there anymore to monitor each other. All in all, when you're on your own, it's harder to be consistent. Every time you give in, you feel like the other parent is the one who's going to have to pay for it later on, or at least to split the bill with you, and suddenly the cost seems more tolerable. A bit like throwing a cigarette butt on the stairway versus throwing it inside your own home. And now that they don't have a home anymore—meaning that they don't have the same one—they litter, big-time.

I want to I want to I want to I want to I want to I want to I want to I want to I want to I want to I want to I want to I want to I want to I want to I want to

One of the programs Hillel loves to watch when he's with Gilad is a Japanese cartoon series about a little boy with magic powers, whose name is Tony. This boy's mother, who is a fairy, taught him once that if he just closed his eyes and kept saying "I want to," all his wishes would come true. Sometimes it takes less than a second for Tony's dream to come true, and if that doesn't happen, his mother the fairy explains that it isn't because he's failed but simply because he stopped saying "I want to" too soon. Tony could go through almost a whole chapter with his eyes closed and "I want to I want to I want to" without giving up, until the magic worked. As far as the production costs were concerned, the idea was very economical, because in every chapter you could recycle the shot with Tony, the bead of sweat gleaming on his forehead, mumbling over and over again, "I want to I want to I want to." The same shot, over and over, in every episode. You can go nuts just sitting there and watching it, but Hillel can't take his eyes off the screen.

I want to I want to I want to I want to I want to I want to I want to I want to I want to I want to I want to I want to I want to I want to I want to I want to I want to

Gilad is smiling again. "It won't do any good, Hilleli," he says. "Even if you say it a million times, it won't do any good. We can't take the bus to kindergarten, because it's just too close. It's right here, at the end of the street. And there's no bus that goes there."

"It will too," Hillel says, and even though he's stopped droning, his eyes stay shut and his forehead stays wrinkled. "Really, Daddy. It will. I just stopped too soon." Gilad was about to take advantage of the window of opportunity in the droning to sneak in a tempting proposition. A bribe. A Snickers bar, maybe. There's a grocery store right next to the kindergarten. Naama doesn't allow candy bars in the morning, but he doesn't care now. Naama won't allow it, and Gilad will. There are extenuating circumstances. The thoughts rush through his mind, but before Gilad has a chance to offer the Snickers bar, Hillel is at it again.

I want to I want to I want to I want to I want to I want to I want to I want to I want to I want to I want to I want to I want to I want to I want to I want to

Gilad announces the Snickers. He repeats this several times. Snickers. Snickers. Snick-ers. At the top of his voice. Close to Hillel's ear. If Naama were there, she'd tell Gilad to stop shouting at him and she'd look horrified. That's something she's good at—looking horrified. Making him feel at any given moment that he's an abusive father or a lousy husband or just a shitty human being. And that's a kind of talent too. A magical power. Weak magic, true, weak and nerve-racking, but still it's magic. And what magic powers can Gilad display? None. One magican mother, one magician kid, one father with no powers at all. A Japanese series. It can go on like this forever.

I want to I want to I want to I want to I want to I want to I want to I want to I want to I want to I want to I want to I want to I want to I want to I want to

Gilad holds Hillel tight in both arms, hoists him in the air, and starts running. Hillel is warm, the way he always is. Even now, he keeps muttering, but as soon as Gilad starts holding him close the muttering turns calmer and the furrows in his forehead disappear. Gilad feels he ought to be muttering something too, together with Hillel. He starts with "We're going to kindergarten we're going to kindergarten," and halfway there he shifts to "We'll be there soon we'll be there soon we'll be there soon," and when they're really close to the yard and to the locked electric gate it suddenly turns into "Daddy loves Daddy loves Daddy loves." It has nothing to do with anything, and the sentence doesn't have an object even though it's obvious, to Gilad at least, that he means he loves Hillel.

As they enter the kindergarten, he stops muttering and puts Hillel down on the ground. Hillel continues, his eyes shut: "I want to I want to I want to." Gilad smiles at one of the teacher's aides, a chubby lady he happens to like, and hangs Hillel's embroidered bag, with the extra set of clothes and the plastic bottle, on the hook where it says HILLEL. He begins making his way out when the kindergarten teacher stops him.

I want to I want to I want to I want to I want to I want to I want to I want to I want to I want to I want to I want to I want to I want to I want to I want to

Gilad smiles at her. He's perspiring after the run and panting a bit too, but his smile says everything is fine. "It's something Hillel saw on television last night," he explains. "This series—Tony and the magic butterflies. Something Japanese. Children are crazy for it . . ." The teacher shushes him the way he's seen her do with misbehaving children. It's insulting, but he prefers not to react. All he wants is to get out of there. And the calmer and nicer he is—he figures—the sooner he'll be able to leave. And he can always tell the kindergarten teacher about some meeting at the office or something. After all, she knows he's a lawyer.

I want to I want to I want to I want to I want to I want to I want to I want to I want to I want to I want to I want to I want to I want to I want to I want to I want to

The teacher tries to talk to Hillel. She even touches him on the face gently, but Hillel doesn't stop muttering and doesn't open his eyes. Gilad's instinct is to tell her it won't do any good, but he's not sure this is going to work in his favor. Maybe now, he thinks to himself, maybe now is the right moment to mention the meeting at the office and to simply leave.

I want to I want to I want to I want to I want to I want to I want to I want to I want to I want to I want to I want to I want to I want to I want to I want to I want to

"I'm sorry," the teacher says. "You can't leave him here in this state." Gilad tries to explain it's not a state. It's just some garbage they show on television, it's like a game. It isn't like the child is suffering or anything. He's just obsessed with this nonsense. But the teacher won't listen and Gilad has no choice other than to pick Hillel up again. The teacher walks them out, and as she opens the gate for them she says in an empathic tone that it might be a good idea to phone Naama because this isn't something they can ignore, and Gilad agrees with her at once and says he'll take care of it, mainly because he's afraid she'll call Naama herself.

I want to I want to I want to I want to I want to I want to I want to I want to I want to I want to I want to I want to I want to I want to I want to I want to I want to I want to

Once they're outside, Gilad puts Hillel down on the sidewalk and says in a fairly quiet tone, "Which bus?" And as Hillel goes right on muttering, he repeats his question louder: "Which bus?" Hillel stops, opens his eyes, gives Gilad a penetrating look, and says, "A big blue bus." Gilad nods and, trying to sound completely normal, completely without tears, he asks whether it matters which number the bus has. And Hillel smiles and shakes his head.

They walk toward Dizengoff Street and wait at the bus stop. The first one that arrives is red. They don't get on. But right after that another one pulls up. It's big and blue. Bus number 1 to Abu Kabir. While Gilad buys the ticket, Hillel waits patiently, the way he promised he would, and then makes his way carefully down the aisle, holding on to the poles. They sit down in the back, next to each other. The bus is completely empty. Gilad tries to remember the last time he was in Abu Kabir. It was when he was still doing his internship and someone in the office sent him to the Forensic Institute there to photocopy an autopsy report. That was before he realized that criminal law was not for him. Hillel wanted to know if this bus went to the kindergarten and Gilad said more or less, or that metaphorically speaking it did, eventually. If Hillel had asked what *metaphorically* meant, the way he sometimes did when he came across words like that, he'd have a problem. But Hillel didn't ask. He just put his little hand on Gilad's thigh and looked out the window. Gilad leaned back, shut his eyes, and tried not to think about anything. The wind through the open window was strong, but not too strong. His body was breathing slowly and his lips weren't moving at all, but in his heart he kept saying: "I want to I want to I want to I want to I want to I want to."

HEMORRHOID

This is the story of a man who suffered from a hemorrhoid. Not a lot of hemorrhoids. A single, solitary one. This hemorrhoid started out small and annoying, but very soon it became medium-sized and irritating, and in less than two months it grew to be big and really painful. The man continued to live his life as usual: he worked long hours every day, took time off on weekends, and fucked on the side whenever he had the chance. But this hemorrhoid, which was clinging to a vein, kept reminding him at every long meeting or through every painful bowel movement that to live is to suffer, to live is to sweat, to live is an ache you can't fucking forget. And so, before every important decision, the man would listen to his hemorrhoid the way others listen to their conscience. And the hemorrhoid, like any hemorrhoid, would give the man some asshole advice. Advice on whom to fire, advice on aiming higher, advice on whether to pick a fight and with whom he should conspire. And it worked. With every passing day, the man became more and more successful. The earnings of the company he ran kept growing, and so did the hemorrhoid. It reached a point where the hemorrhoid outgrew the man. And even then, it didn't stop. Until eventually it was the hemorrhoid that was chairman of the board. And sometimes, when the hemorrhoid took its seat on the chair in the boardroom, it found the man underneath a little irritating.

This is the story of a hemorrhoid that suffered from a man. The hemorrhoid continued to live its life as usual: It worked long hours every day, took time off on weekends, and fucked on the side whenever it had the chance. But this man, who was clinging to a vein, kept reminding him at every long meeting or painful BM that to live is to yearn, to live is to burn, to live is to fucking screw up and wait for fate to turn. And the hemorrhoid would listen to the man the way people listen to their stomach when it rumbles and asks for food— passively but acceptingly. And thanks to this man, the hemorrhoid tried to believe it could live and let live, it could learn to forgive. It could conquer its urge to look down on others. And even when it swore, it didn't mention people's mothers. And so, thanks to the irritating little man under him, everyone came to value the hemorrhoid: hemorrhoids, people, and, of course, the company's satisfied shareholders all around the world.

SEPTEMBER ALL YEAR LONG

When the new great depression began, NW was hardest hit. Its merchandise was meant for the affluent class, but after the Chicago riots, even the wealthy stopped ordering, some of them because of the unstable economic situation, but most of them because they just couldn't face their neighbors. The shares lay on the stock-market floors of the world and bled out, percentage after percentage. And NW turned into a symbol of the depression. The headline of *The Wall Street Journal*'s story about it was "Hailstorms in September," a takeoff of its ad "September All Year Long," which showed a family clad only in bathing suits on a sunny autumn day decorating a Christmas tree. The ad caught on like wildfire. A week after it was broadcast for the first time, they were already selling three thousand units a day. Wealthy Americans bought, and so did the less wealthy who were faking it. The NW weather-control systems became a status symbol. The official stamp of a millionaire. They now signified what executive jets used to signify in the '90s and into 2000. Nice Weather, weather for the wealthy. If you live in Arctic Greenland, and the snow and grayness are driving you crazy, all you have to do is swipe your credit card and, with a satellite or two, they'll set you up with a perfect autumn day in Cannes on your balcony every day of the year.

Yakov (Yaki) Brayk was one of the first to buy the system from them. He truly loved his money and had a hard time parting with it, but even more than he loved the millions he earned from selling weapons and drugs to Zimbabwe, he hated those humid New York summers and that icky feeling when your sweaty undershirt sticks to your back. He bought a system not only for himself but for the whole block. Some people mistakenly saw that as generosity, but the truth is he did it just to keep the great weather with him all the way to the corner convenience store. That convenience store wasn't only the place to buy unfiltered Noblesse cigarettes they imported from Israel for him; more than anything, it marked for Yaki the boundary of his living space. And from the minute Yaki signed the check, the block turned into a weather paradise. No dismal rain or sweltering heat. Just September all year long. And not, God forbid, that annoying New York September, but the kind he grew up with in Haifa. And then suddenly, out of the blue, there were the riots in Chicago and the neighbors demanded that he turn off his perfect autumn weather. At first, he ignored them, but then those lawyers' letters turned up in his mailbox and someone left a slaughtered peacock on his windshield. That's when his wife asked him to turn it off. It was January. Yaki turned off the autumn and the day instantly became shorter and sadder. All because of one slaughtered peacock and an anxiety-ridden, anorexic wife who, as always, was able to control him through her weakness.

The recession just got worse. On Wall Street, NW stocks hit rock bottom, and so did shares in Yaki's company. And after they hit rock bottom, they drilled a hole through the rocks and fell even lower. It's funny, you'd think that weapons and drugs would be recessionproof, but actually the opposite turned out to be true. People had no money to buy medicine and they rediscovered what they'd long forgotten: that live weapons are a luxury, just like electric car windows, and that sometimes it takes only a stone you found in the yard to smash somebody's skull in. They quickly learned to manage without Yaki's rifles, much more quickly than Yaki could get used to the gloomy weather of mid-March. And Yaki Brayk, or Lucky Brayk, as the financial columnists liked to call him, went bankrupt.

He kept the apartment (the company's accountant managed to retroactively put it in the anorexic's wife's name), but all the rest was gone. They even took the furniture. Four days later, an NW technician came to disconnect the system. When Yaki opened the door for him, he was standing there completely rain-soaked. Yaki made him hot coffee and they talked for a while. Yaki told him that not long after the Chicago riot, he'd stopped using the system. The technician said that a lot of customers had stopped. They talked about the riot, when a furious mob from the slums stormed the summery homes of the wealthy residents of the city. "All that sun they had drove us crazy," one of the rioters said on a news commentary show a few days later. "Let's see you freezing your butt off with no money for heat and those bastards, those bastards . . ." At that point, he burst into tears. The camera blurred his face to hide his identity, so you couldn't actually see the tears, but you could hear him wailing like a wounded animal. The technician, who was black, said he was born in that neighborhood in Chicago, but today he was ashamed to admit it. "That money," he said, "all that fucking money just fucked up the world."

After coffee, when the technician was ready to disconnect the system, Yaki asked if he could turn it on just one last time. The technician shrugged and Yaki took that as a yes. He pressed a few buttons on the remote and the sun suddenly came out from behind a cloud. "That's not the real sun, you know," the technician said proudly. "What they do is image it, with lasers." Yaki winked and said, "Don't spoil it. For me, it's the sun." The technician nodded and said, "A great sun. Too bad you can't keep it out till I get back to the car. I'm sick of this rain." Yaki didn't answer. He just closed his eyes and let the sun wash over his face.

JOSEPH

There are conversations that can change a person's life. I'm sure of it. I mean, I'd like to believe it. I'm sitting in a café with a producer. He's not exactly a producer, he never produced anything, but he wants to. He has an idea for a film and he wants me to write the screenplay. I explain that I don't write for films, and he accepts that and calls the waitress over. I'm sure he wants to ask for the check, but he orders himself another espresso instead. The waitress asks me if I want something else, and I ask for a glass of water. The wannabe producer's name is Yossef, but he introduces himself as Joseph. "No one," he says, "is really called Yossef. It's always Sefi or Yossi or Yoss, so I went for Joseph." He's sharp, that Joseph. Reads me like a book. "You're busy, right?" he says when he sees me glance at my watch, and immediately adds, "Very busy. Traveling, working, writing e-mails." There's nothing malicious or sarcastic in the way he says it. It's a statement of fact or, at the most, an expression of sympathy. I nod. "Not being busy scares you?" he asks. I nod again. "Me too," he says and gives me a yellow-toothed smile. "There must be something down there. Something frightening. If not, we wouldn't be grinding our time so thin on all kinds of projects. And you know what scares me most?" he asks. I hesitate for a second, thinking about what to answer, but Joseph doesn't wait. "Myself," he continues, "what I am. You know that nothingness that fills you up a second after you come? Not with someone you love, just with some girl, or when you jerk off. You know it? That's what scares me, looking into myself and finding nothing there. Not your average nothingness, but the kind that totally bums you out, I don't know exactly what to call it . . ."

Now he's quiet. I feel uncomfortable with his silence. If we were closer, maybe I could be silent with him. But not at our first meeting. Not after a comment like that. "Sometimes," I say, trying to return his frankness, "life seems like a trap to me. Something you walk into unsuspectingly and then it snaps closed around you. And when you're inside—inside life, I mean—there's no escape, except maybe suicide, which isn't really an escape, it's more like surrender. You know what I mean?"

"It's fuck-all," Joseph says. "It's just fuck-all that you won't write the screenplay." There's something very weird about the way he talks. He doesn't even curse like other people. I don't know what to say after that, so I keep quiet. "Never mind," he says after a minute. "Your saying no just gives me the chance to meet with other people, drink more coffee. And that's the best part of this business. I don't think the actual producing is for me." I must have nodded, because he reacts to it. "You think I don't have it, right? That I'm not really a producer, that I'm just some guy with a little money from his parents who talks a lot." I must still be nodding, unintentionally, from the pressure, because now he's laughing. "You're right," he says, "or maybe not, maybe I'll surprise you yet. And myself."

Joseph asks for the check and insists on paying. "What

about our waitress?" he asks while we wait for his credit card to be swiped. "You figure she's trying to escape too? From herself, I mean?" I shrug. "And that guy who just walked in, with the coat? Look how he's sweating. He's definitely running away from something. Maybe we'll form a start-up. Instead of the film—a program that finds people who are trying to run away from themselves, who are afraid of what they might find out. It could be a hit." I look at the sweaty guy in the coat. It's the first time in my life I see a suicide bomber. Afterward, in the hospital, foreign journalists will ask me to describe him and I'll say I don't remember. Because I'll think it's something kind of personal, something I should keep between me and him. Joseph will survive the blast too. But not so the waitress. Not that there's any culpability on her part. In terrorist attacks, character is not a factor. In the end, it's all a matter of angle and distance. "That guy who just came in is definitely running away from something," Joseph says, and laughs, rummaging around in his pockets for some change for the tip. "Maybe he'll agree to write the screenplay for me or at least meet for coffee." Our waitress, laminated menu in hand, dances her way over to the sweaty guy in the coat.

MOURNERS' MEAL

She decided to open the restaurant right away, the morning after the funeral. When Itamar heard about it, she thought he'd explode. "Just one hour ago you buried your husband, and already you're in a hurry to sell çorba?!" "We don't do çorba, Itamar," Halina said in her most reassuring voice, "and it's not about money at all. It's about people. I do better being with clients at the restaurant than sitting at home on my own." "But you're the one who insisted we shouldn't sit shiva," Itamar said. "You said you didn't want all the hassle." "It wasn't because of the hassle," Halina protested. "When people leave their body to science, you don't sit shiva. That's just how it is. When Horshovsky's father died, nobody . . ." "Give me a break, Mother," Itamar snapped. "Leave Horshovsky out of this, and the Shiffermans and Mrs. Pinchevsky from Twenty-one Bialik Street. Just us, okay? Does it seem reasonable to you that the day after Dad dies you go and open the restaurant as if it were business as usual"? "Yes," Halina insisted. "In my heart, it won't be as usual, but for everyone who comes into the restaurant it will be. Your father may be dead, but the business is alive." "The business is dead too," Itamar said, gritting his teeth. "It's been dead for years now. We haven't had so much as a dog in here."

At the hospital, when they told her Gideon had died, she didn't cry. But after what Itamar said, she did. Not in front of him, of course; as long as he was around, she kept a stiff upper lip. But as soon as he left, she cried like a baby. "It doesn't mean I'm not a good wife," she assured herself between sobs. "I'm a lot more upset that Gideon is dead than that Itamar said those things, but insults are much easier to cry over." It was true. Ever since they'd moved to the arcade the clientele had dwindled. She'd been against the move from the word *go*, but Gideon said it was their big chance, "the chance of a life-time." Ever since then, every time they fought, she'd remind him of that "chance of a lifetime," and now that he was dead, there was nobody for her to remind. She and the Chinaman had been sitting in the empty restaurant for three hours in complete silence. The Chinaman had been very fond of Gideon, who was very patient with him. Gideon used to spend hours teaching the Chinaman how to make cholent and gefilte fish, and whenever he ruined anything, and Halina would blurt out a swearword, Gideon would intervene: "Never mind, never mind." If nobody shows up by three, she'll close, she thought. Not just for today. For good. Two people running a business is different. When there's a crowd there's someone to help out, and when there isn't, at least you have someone to talk to. "You okay?" the Chinaman asked, and Halina nodded and tried to smile. Maybe even before three. She'll just lock up and leave.

There were almost twenty of them, and as soon as they stood by the door looking at the menu outside she knew there'd be a racket. The one who came in first was gigantic, a head taller than she was, with salt-and-pepper hair and eye-brows like a carpet. "You open?" he asked, and for a second she debated, but by the time she'd opened her mouth to answer, the restaurant was packed— with gold-and-purple nail polish, and the sharp smell of vodka, and shrieking children. She and the Chinaman lined up a few tables, and when she brought them the menus the tall guy said, "We don't need menus now, lady. Just bring everyone plate and knife-and-fork." And while she and the Chinaman were setting out the plates she spotted the picnic coolers. They started pulling out food and bottles of drink and filling plates, looking not in the least embarrassed. If Gideon were alive, he'd have kicked them out, but she didn't even have it in her to say anything. "Now you come here with us," the tall man said. She signaled the Chinaman to sit down at the table with them, and sat down herself, though she wasn't really in the mood. "Drink up, lady," he commanded. "Drink up." He filled her glass with vodka. "Today is special day." And as she stared at him, puzzled, he added with a wink: "Today is day we find this restaurant you manage with Japanese guy. Why you not eating?"

Their food was tasty. And after downing a glass or two, Halina didn't mind their coarseness anymore. Even if they weren't ordering anything and even if they were using up all the dishes, she was glad they had come, filling the whole place with their shrieking and their laughter. That way at least she didn't have to stay there on her own. They drank l'chaim—to life. To her life, and to the life of the business, and even to the life of Gideon. For some reason that she couldn't quite figure out, she told them he was abroad on business. Then they drank to the life of Gideon's business abroad and to Joseph, which was what they called the Chinaman. And to the life of Joseph's family and then to the life of the state. And Halina, who was a bit drunk by then, tried to remember how many years it had been since she'd last toasted the state. When they finished everything in their picnic coolers, the tall guy asked her what she thought of their food, and Halina said it was excellent. "Very good," the tall guy smiled. "I'm happy. And now, we have your menu." At first, Halina didn't understand what he meant. Maybe because of the vodka. But the tall guy explained right away: "You sat with us and you ate our food. Now it is time for us to sit with you and eat your food."

They ordered from the menu as if they hadn't eaten a thing, and ate voraciously. Salads, soups, pot roasts, and, afterward, even dessert. "Your food is good, lady," the tall guy said, taking out his wallet to pay. "Very good. Even better than what we bring." And when he'd finished counting the bills and putting them on the table, he added: "Your husband, when he is coming back?" Halina hesitated before answering, and then said it wasn't clear yet and that it all depended on his business over there. "He left wife behind, alone?" the tall guy said disapprovingly, his voice kind of sad. "That is not right." And Halina, who wanted to say everything was fine and that she was managing, really, found herself nodding, and smiling, as if her eyes weren't glistening with tears.

PARALLEL UNIVERSES

There's a theory that says there are billions of other universes, parallel to the one we live in, and that each of them is slightly different. There are the ones where you were never born, and the ones where you wouldn't want to be born. There are some parallel universes where I'm having sex with a horse, and ones where I win the lottery. There are universes where I'm lying on the bedroom floor, slowly bleeding to death, and universes where I've been elected president, by a landslide. But I don't care about any of those parallel universes now. The only ones that interest me are the ones where she isn't happily married, with a cute little boy, the ones where she's completely alone. There are plenty of universes like that, I'm sure. I'm trying to think about them now. Among all those universes, there are some where we've never met. I don't care about those now. Among the ones that are left, there are some where she doesn't want me. She tells me no. In some of them, she does it gently, and in others—in a way that hurts. I don't care about those now, either. All that's left are the ones where she tells me yes, and I choose one of them, a little like you choose a piece of fruit at the greengrocer's. I choose the nicest one, the ripest one, the sweetest one. It's a universe where the weather is perfect, never too hot or too cold, and we live there in a little cottage in the woods. She works at the city library, a forty-minute drive from our home, and I work in the education department of the regional council, in the building that faces hers. Sometimes, from my office window, I can see her putting books back on the shelf. We always have our lunch together. And I love her and she loves me. And I love her and she loves me. And I love her and she loves me. I'd give anything to move to that universe. But meanwhile, until I find the way there, all I can do is think about it. I picture myself living there, in the middle of the woods. With her, in complete happiness. There's an infinite number of parallel universes in the world. In one of them, I'm having sex with a horse; in another, I win the lottery. I don't want to think about those now, only about that one, the one with the cottage in the woods. There's a universe where I'm lying with my wrists slashed, bleeding, on the bedroom floor. That's the universe I'm doomed to live in until it's over. I don't want to think about it now. I just want to think about that other universe. A cottage in the woods, the sun setting, going to bed early. In bed, my right arm is unslashed, and dry. She's lying on it and we're hugging each other. She lies on it for so long that I can hardly feel it anymore. But I don't move, I like it that way, with my arm under her warm body, and I keep liking it even when I can no longer feel my arm at all. I can sense her breathing on my face—rhythmic, regular, unending. My eyes begin to shut. Not just in that universe, in bed, in the woods, but in the other universes too, the ones that I don't want to think about. I enjoy knowing there's one place, in the heart of the woods, where I'm falling asleep happy.

UPGRADE

I talk too much. Sometimes when I'm talking and talking and talking that moment arrives—right there in the middle of the conversation—when I notice the person next to me has long stopped listening. He may keep up the nodding, but his eyes—they've completely clouded over. His mind has wandered, and he's thinking thoughts sweeter than the ones I share.

Of course, I could take issue with that assumption. I can pretty much argue anything. My wife says I'd get philosophical with a lamppost if I thought the thing had ears. I could've argued the point with the guy sitting next to me—but there's no joy in it. He's already stopped listening. He's in another world. A better one (at least, in his opinion it is). And me? I keep on talking and talking and talking. It's like a car with the hand brake yanked: The wheels lock but it just goes on skidding down the road.

I want to stop talking. I do! But the words, the sentences, the ideas, there's a momentum to them, it's impossible to just stop them in their tracks, to seal up the lips and halt the words, right there, mid-sentence. There are people capable of doing it, I know.

Mainly women.

And when they go silent, it makes whoever's listening feel guilty. It spurs in the listener a yearning, a deep need to lean forward and hug them and say, "I'm sorry."

To say, "I love you."

I'd give up an eyeball to be able to do it, anything to have what it takes for that kind of on-a-dime stoppage. I'd make use of that gift, right nice. I'd up and stop speaking next to the girls that truly rate, and they'd just want to hug me, to squeeze me and say, "I love you." And even if they didn't actually do it, the fact that they'd wanted to would still be worth something. Worth a lot.

On this specific day, I can't stop talking next to a guy by the name of Michael. He's a graphic designer for a Hasidic newspaper in Brooklyn, flying from New York to Louisville, Kentucky, to sit in his uncle's sukkah. He's not especially close to this uncle, and not especially keen on Louisville. But his uncle sent him the ticket as a gift, and Michael is just plain wild about the frequent-flier points. He's got a trip to Australia coming up, and with the points from the Louisville leg he'll be able to upgrade to Business. On long flights, Michael tells me, the difference between Business and Coach, it's just day and night.

"What do you prefer," I ask him, "day or night?"

Because me, generally, I'm the night type, but the day also has something special about it, a radiance. At night it's quieter and colder, which is a significant consideration, at least for me, living as I do in tropical climes. But at night you're also liable to feel more alone if you don't have someone at your side, if you get my meaning . . . the one that I'm insinuating.

"I don't," Michael says, his tone turned sharp.

"I'm not gay," I tell him. Because I can see I've got him

stressed. "All this talk about loneliness and nighttime sounds pretty much like textbook gay talk, I know it. But I'm not. I've kissed a guy on the mouth only once, and that's in the whole thirty-plus years of my life, and even that was half by accident. This was back when I was in the army. There was a soldier by the name of Tzlil Drucker in my unit, and he'd brought some hash to the base, and suggested we smoke it. Tzlil asked if I'd ever smoked before, and I said yes, I had. I hadn't intended to lie, it's just I've got a natural propensity for it. So pretty much when anyone asks me for anything and I'm under pressure I always answer yes. Just—you know—to appease. It's a reflex that has the potential to complicate things for me, big-time. Picture this: A cop walks into a room, sees me standing next to a corpse, and asks, "Did you murder him?" That one's liable to end badly. The same cop could also ask me something like "Are you innocent?" In that case, I'd come out of it all right. But really, between us, what're the chances that a policeman's going to ask it like that?

So Tzlil and I smoked together, and it was a completely unique sensation. The drug, it just shut my mouth—plugged it up completely. I didn't have to speak in order to just be. And during it, Tzlil told me that a year had gone by since he'd broken up with his girlfriend. That a year had gone by from the last time he'd kissed a woman. I remember he used that word, *woman*. I told him that I'd never kissed a woman, or even a girl.

"On the mouth is what I meant. On the cheek I'd kissed bunches. Aunties and the like. Anyway, Tzlil stared at me without saying a word, but I could see he was surprised. And then suddenly we were kissing. His tongue was rough and tangy, sort of like if you licked a rusty rail on the boardwalk. And I remember thinking back then, thinking that all the tongues and all the kisses that would ever be mine were going to feel just like that. And I also thought that never having kissed anyone until that day in my life, well, in essence, I hadn't missed a thing.

"Tzlil said, 'I'm not a homo.'

"And I laughed and said, 'But your name is just fantastically gay.'

"And that was that, basically.

"Eight years later, I bumped into him in some random hummus place and when I called him Tzlil he said he didn't go by that anymore and that he'd gone down to the Ministry of the Interior and changed his name to Tzahi.

"'I hope it wasn't on my account.'"

Michael, who's sitting next to me, has long stopped listening. At the beginning, I thought he was all wound up because of the confusion about me coming on to him. Afterward I began to suspect that he was actually gay, and that I'd insulted him with my story, that it was as if I were saying that kissing guys is gross. But when I look him in the eye, I find neither insult nor anxiety— just a bunch of frequent-flier points accumulating toward an upgrade, toward more kindly flight attendants, toward higher-quality coffee and enough legroom for a man to really stretch out.

When I see this, I feel guilty.

It isn't the first time I've seen that in the eyes of someone I'm talking to, and I don't mean the legroom thing. I'm referring to the not-listening part—seeing that a person is thinking about something else completely. Always, I feel guilty. My wife says I shouldn't feel guilty, especially when my talking too much is so obviously a cry for help. She says the specific words coming out of my mouth don't matter at all, because what I'm really saying at any given moment is simply "Help!" Think about it, she says. You're there screaming "Help!" and meanwhile they're thinking about something else. If anyone is supposed to feel guilty, it should be them, not you.

My wife's tongue is smooth and pleasant. Her tongue is the best place to be in the whole wide world. If it were only a little bit wider and a little bit longer, I'd move in for good. I'd roll myself up into that tongue—I'd be the crab to her California roll, the eel to her eel-and-avocado. I tell you, thinking back to the tongue I started my kissing with and then looking at the tongue I ended up with, it wouldn't be unfair to say that I've really made something of this life of mine. That I've managed my own little *combina* of an upgrade.

Truth be told, I've never once flown Business Class. But if the difference between that and Coach is anything like the difference between my wife's tongue and the one in the mouth of Tzahi-Tzlil Drucker, I'd be ready to spend a week living in the coldest, dampest sukkah in the world with the stiffest, most boring uncle for the chance to get that kind of upgrade.

They announce overhead that we'll be landing in a little bit. I keep talking. Michael keeps not listening. Planet Earth keeps spinning on its axis. Just another four days, my love. Another four days and I return to you. Another four days and, once again, I'll find it in my heart to shut up.

GUAVA

There was no sound from the engines of the plane. There were no sounds at all. Except perhaps the soft crying of the flight attendants a few rows behind him. Through the elliptical window, Shkedi looked at the cloud hovering just below him. He could imagine the plane dropping through it like a stone, punching an enormous hole that would be sealed again quickly with the first breeze, leaving not so much as a scar. "Just don't crash," Shkedi said. "Just don't crash."

Forty seconds before Shkedi expired, an angel appeared, all dressed in white, and told him he'd been awarded a last wish. Shkedi tried to find out what *awarded* implied. Was it an award like winning the lottery or was it something a bit more flattering: awarded in the sense of an achievement, in recognition of his good deeds? The angel shrugged. "Beats me," he said with pure angelic sincerity. "They told me to come and fulfill, on the double. They didn't say why." "That's a shame," Shkedi said. "Because it's absolutely fascinating. Especially now when I'm about to leave this world and all, I'd really like to know if I'm leaving it as just another lucky guy or if I'm leaving it with a pat on the back." "Forty seconds and you kick off," the angel droned. "If you want to spend those forty seconds yapping, that's fine with me. No problem. Just consider that your window of opportunity is about to close." Shkedi considered, and quickly made his wish. But not before taking the trouble to point out to the angel that he had a strange way of talking. For an angel, that is. The angel was hurt. "What do you mean, 'for an angel'? Have you ever heard an angel talk, that you dump a thing like that on me?" "Never," Shkedi admitted. Suddenly, the angel looked much less angelic and much less pleasant, but that was nothing compared with what he looked like after he heard the wish.

"Peace on earth?" he screamed. "Peace on earth? You're kidding me!"

And then Shkedi died.

Shkedi was dead and the angel was left behind. Left behind with the most bothersome and complicated wish he'd ever been asked to fulfill. Mostly, people ask for a new car for the wife, an apartment for the kid. Reasonable stuff. Specific stuff. But peace on earth is one hell of a job. First, the guy bugs him with questions like he's the AT&T directory, then he has the audacity to put down the way he talks, and to top it off, he lands him with peace on earth. If Shkedi hadn't kicked off, the angel would have stuck to him like herpes, and wouldn't have let go till he changed his wish. But the guy's soul was in seventh heaven by now, and who knows how he'd ever find it.

The angel took a deep breath. "Peace on earth, that's all," he mumbled. "Just peace on earth, that's all."

And while all this was going on, Shkedi's soul completely forgot it had ever belonged to a person called Shkedi, and was reincarnated, pure and untainted, secondhand but good as new, as a piece of fruit. Yes, a piece of fruit. A guava.

The new soul had no thoughts. A guava doesn't have thoughts. But it had feelings. It felt an overwhelming fear. It was afraid of falling off the tree. Not that it had the words to describe this fear. But if it had, it would have been something like "Oh my God!" And while it was hanging there, on the tree, petrified, peace began to reign on earth. People beat their swords into plowshares and nuclear reactors soon began to be used for peaceful purposes. But none of this was of any comfort to the guava. Because the tree was tall and the ground seemed distant and painful. Just don't crash, the guava shuddered wordlessly, just don't crash.

SURPRISE PARTY

Three people are waiting at an intercom. A weird moment. More precisely, an awkward moment, uncomfortable.

"You're here for Avner's birthday too?" one of them, a guy with a graying mustache, asks the guy who pressed the buzzer. The guy who pressed the buzzer nods. The third one, tall with a Band-Aid on his nose, nods too. "No kidding." Mustache massages his neck nervously. "You're friends of his?" They both nod. A female voice rings out from the intercom.

"Come on up, the twenty-first floor," and then the buzz that opens the door. The elevator buttons only go up to 21; our Avner lives in the penthouse.

On the way up, Mustache confesses that he doesn't really know Avner. Mustache is just the manager of the bank in Ramat Aviv where Avner and Pnina Katzman have an account. He has never met them, didn't start at that branch till two months ago. Before that he managed a smaller branch in Ra'anana. That's why he was surprised when Pnina called to invite him to this party, but she insisted, said that Avner would be so happy.

Band-Aid-on-the-Nose, it turns out, isn't really a close friend either. He's the husband's insurance agent, only met him a couple of times. And that was a while ago. For the last few years, they've been doing all their business by e-mail.

The guy who pressed the buzzer, nice-looking, but with connected eyebrows, knows the Katzmans best. He's their dentist. He filled four cavities for Pnina and made a crown for one of her molars. He also worked on Avner's teeth, filled one cavity and did a root canal, but he wouldn't really call himself a friend.

"It's strange that she invited us," Mustache says.

"It's probably a big party," Band-Aid decides.

"I wasn't planning to come," Eyebrows admits, "but Pnina is so sensitive."

"Is she pretty?" Mustache asks. That's not a question a bank manager should ask, he knows. Eyebrows nods and shrugs at the same time as if to say, "Yes, but what good will that do us?"

Pnina really is pretty. She's forty-plus and looks it. No face-lifts to keep the wrinkles away. If you could match a particular male sexual fantasy to every woman, Mustache thinks as he shakes her limp hand, then Pnina would be the perfect damsel in distress. There's a certain lack of confidence about her, a helplessness. Apart from the three of them, it turns out, no one has shown up yet. Just the catering staff, who are putting out more and more giant aluminum-covered bowls and trays jam-packed with hors d'oeuvres. No, Pnina assures them, they're not early. It's just the others who are late.

"It's my fault," she explains. "I decided on everything at the last minute. That's why I didn't invite any of you till today. I apologize." Mustache says she has nothing to apologize for.

Eyebrows is already standing over one of the trays, getting to work on the bruschetta. So beautifully are they arranged that every one he takes is made conspicuous by its absence, like a pulled tooth.

He knows it's not very polite and he should wait for the rest of the guests, but he's dying of hunger. He operated on an old man's upper and lower gums today, a three-and-a-half-hour procedure, then he just changed clothes and took off for this party. He didn't even have time to go home first. He's hungry now, hungry and embarrassed. The bruschetta is good. He takes another one, his fifth, and walks off to stand at the side.

The living room of the apartment is absolutely enormous, and there's also a glass door leading to the roof. Pnina tells them that she invited three hundred people, everyone she found listed in Avner's BlackBerry. Not all of them are coming, she knows, definitely not at such short notice, but it's going to be such fun.

The last time she organized a surprise party was ten years ago. They were living in India then because of Avner's business, and one of the guests brought them a lion cub as a gift. In India, it seems, they're more flexible about laws for the preservation of wildlife, or maybe they just obey them less. That lion cub was the most adorable thing Pnina had ever seen in her life. In fact, that whole party was a tremendous success. Not that she's expecting anyone to bring them a lion today, but people are coming and they'll drink and laugh together, and it'll just be such fun.

"Letting ourselves go like that is just what we all need, especially Avner, who's been working like a dog on the stock issue for the last few months," Pnina says.

That story about India reminds Mustache of something—he brought a gift too. He reaches into his pocket and takes out a long box wrapped in colored paper imprinted with the bank's logo.

"It's just a little something," he says in an apologetic tone, "and it's not from me, it's from the entire branch."

Anyway, it's hard to give a gift after such an amazing story about a lion. Pnina says thank you and hugs Mustache—a rather surprising gesture, considering they don't know each other. That, at least, is what Band-Aid thinks. Pnina insists that Mustache hold on to the gift for the time being and give it to Avner personally.

She's sure, she says, that Avner will be so happy, he always loves gifts.

That last remark makes Eyebrows feel uncomfortable for not bringing something. Band-Aid didn't bring a gift either, but then again, he isn't eating anything, and Eyebrows has already finished off six bruschetta, two pieces of herring, and some squid sushi, which, as the kid with the tray insisted on pointing out, twice, isn't kosher. Eyebrows knows he shouldn't have come, but now all he can do is wait till Avner and the other guests show up, and then, when everyone is busy partying, make his exit. But meanwhile, he's stuck here, he knows, totally stuck, and in the twenty minutes that have passed since he walked in the door, not one other guest has arrived.

"When did you say that Avner is supposed to get here?" Eyebrows asks, trying to be nonchalant. It doesn't work. Pnina gets upset.

"He should be here by now," she says, "but he doesn't know about the party, so maybe he'll be a little late." She pours Eyebrows a glass of wine. He refuses politely, but she insists.

Band-Aid asks if there's any cognac. That makes Pnina very happy and she totters off to the liquor cabinet in her spike heels and takes out a bottle.

"The catering guys probably have cognac," she says, "but not as good as this. This might not be enough for all the guests, but it is for our intimate little group, so let's make a toast."

She pours cognac for Mustache and herself, too, and they raise their glasses. Mustache, seeing that no one else is planning to say anything, quickly steps into the breach. He wishes all those present many parties and many surprises, nice ones, of course. And to Avner he wishes a speedy arrival, otherwise there won't be anything left for him to eat or drink. He and Pnina laugh.

Eyebrows feels as if that remark is somehow about him. True, he's eaten a lot since he came in, but he still thinks it's kind of nasty for Mustache to sell him out for a joke. And Pnina too—it's insulting, the way she's laughing at that tasteless bit of humor, exposing crowns that wouldn't be there if not for him. That's it, he decides, time to go. He'll do it politely so as not to hurt anyone's feelings, but with all due respect, he has a wife waiting at home, and all this place has to offer is a slightly tense atmosphere and nonkosher sushi.

Pnina's response to Eyebrows's stammered goodbye is extreme. "You can't go," she says, clutching his hand, "this party is so important to Avner, and without you . . . as it is, almost no one else came. But they'll be here"—she pulls herself together quickly—"they probably just got held up on the road, there's heavy traffic at this hour, but if Avner arrives before them, he'll open the door and see only two people. Wonderful people, but only two. Not counting the catering crew, of course. That could be a letdown. And the last thing anyone needs on his fiftieth birthday is a letdown. It's a rough age as it is. And Avner hasn't had an easy time of it these last few months, so the last thing he needs when he comes in is to be welcomed by an empty living room."

"Even three's not a lot," Eyebrows maliciously states the obvious. The truth is, he adds, that if he were Pnina, he'd just cancel the whole thing and try to clear the place before Avner got home.

Pnina is quick to agree. She calls the catering manager over and tells him not to bring up any more food and to take his crew and wait downstairs in their truck for the time being. When the rest of the guests arrive, she'll text them and they can come up again.

Till then, she explains to everyone without letting go of Eyebrows's hand, they'll all sit here in the living room and wait for Avner with a drink.

Maybe she should have planned something a little more intimate from the beginning. After all, fifty is not the age for wild dancing and loud music; fifty is more the age for stimulating conversation with close, insightful friends.

Eyebrows wanted to tell her that none of the people here are close to Avner, but he sees that she's already on the verge of tears and decides to keep quiet and let her drag him to the couch. She sits him down, and Band-Aid and Mustache join them.

Mustache is a world champion calmer-downer. He's already had more than a few conversations in his life with clients who lost all their money after the bottom fell out of one investment or another and he always knows how to act, especially with women. Now he bombards them with jokes, pours them all drinks, puts a comforting hand on Pnina's pale shoulder. If a stranger walked in, he'd probably think they were a couple.

Band-Aid seems pretty much at home too. What he has going for him is that he's in no great hurry to leave. He has a wife who always looks as if someone close to her has died, and an annoying two-year-old kid it's his turn to bathe today.

Here, he can sit around, drink a little, rub shoulders with someone who's had a bit more success in life than him, at least financially, and officially it could even be considered work.

Back home, whenever he gets there, he'll just have to make a tired face and say they talked his head off all evening and all he could do was smile and take it because they're really good clients.

"That's how it is," he'll tell his wife, "to make a living, I have to listen to people's crap just like you have to . . ." and then he'll shut up as if he's forgotten, as if it just slipped his mind that she hasn't worked for more than two years and the entire financial burden falls on him alone.

She'll probably cry then, tell him that the postpartum depression isn't her fault, that it's a scientifically proven illness, that it's not just in her mind, it's chemical, like any other illness. She's dying to go back to work, if only she could, but she can't, she just can't . . . and he'll interrupt her stream of words and apologize, say he didn't mean anything, that the words just slipped out of his mouth. And she'll believe him, or not. With all that wasteland between them, what does it really matter.

Mustache seems to pick up on everything that's going through Band-Aid's mind and pours him a little more cognac.

That Mustache is something, Band-Aid thinks, a special guy. Eyebrows, on the other hand, is kind of neurotic and makes him nervous. When they first got here, he kept eating the whole time and now he just looks at his watch and scratches himself. Before, when Pnina tried to persuade him to stay, he almost wanted to break into the conversation and tell her to leave him alone, to just let him go. No one needs him here. You might think he's Avner's childhood friend or something when he's just some guy who drilled his teeth.

And anyway, when he thinks about it, it's a little strange that they're the only ones who came. What does that say about Avner's really close friends? That they're so egotistical? That he's offended them? Or maybe he doesn't have any?

The intercom buzzes and Pnina runs to answer it. Mustache winks at Eyebrows, and Band-Aid and pours another round of cognac. "Don't worry," he says to Eyebrows, as if he's another customer of the bank who's fallen on bad times, "it'll be fine."

It's just the catering guy on the intercom. Their truck is blocking someone. He asks if he can park in the building parking lot. Before Pnina can answer, the phone rings. She hurries over to pick up the receiver. Silence on the other end.

"Avner," she says, "where are you? Is everything okay?" She knows it's Avner because his number is on the display. But there's no answer on the other end, just the drone of a dead line.

Pnina starts to cry, but it's a weird kind of crying. Her eyes are wet and her whole body trembles, but she doesn't make a sound, like a cell phone on vibrate. Mustache goes right over and takes the cognac glass out of her hand a second before it would have fallen and shattered.

"He's not okay," Pnina says, throwing her arms around Mustache, "something isn't right with him. I knew it, this whole time I knew it. That's why I decided to have the party, to cheer him up."

Mustache takes her to the couch and sits her down next to Eyebrows.

Eyebrows is bummed out. When Pnina came back from answering the phone, he planned to tell her that he had to go. His wife is waiting for him or something, but now he knows he can't. Pnina's sitting so close to him now that he can hear her irregular breathing. And her face is totally pale. It looks like she's going to faint.

Band-Aid brings a glass of water and Mustache puts it to her lips. She drinks a little and starts to calm down.

That was a scary moment, Eyebrows thinks.

I wonder what he said to her on the phone, Band-Aid thinks.

Even when she's weak, Mustache thinks, even when she's on the verge of collapse, she's all woman. Deep in his pants, he feels the beginning of an erection and hopes no one else notices.

The intercom buzzes. It's the catering guy again; he's waiting for an answer about parking in the building parking lot. Traffic's crazy now and finding a spot on the street for a large truck is just impossible. Band-Aid, who answered the buzz, repeats the question out loud.

Mustache gives him a tell-him-it's-okay nod. But the semiconscious Pnina mumbles that he shouldn't use the tenants' parking. There's a neighbor on the seventeenth floor who causes problems. Just last week, an acquaintance who stopped by to see her for an hour, even less, got towed.

Eyebrows volunteers to go downstairs and tell the caterers they can't park in the building lot. From there, he thinks, the way home will be shorter.

Mustache says he should stay, Pnina isn't doing well and

it would be better to have a doctor around. "I'm a doctor of dentistry," Eyebrows says.

"You're a doctor of dentistry, I know," Mustache counters.

Pnina says that they have to go to Avner's office right now. It's not like him to call and then hang up like that. Anyway, something's been wrong with him lately. He's always taking pills. He told Pnina they were for headaches, but Pnina knows headache pills, and what Avner's taking isn't Tylenol or Advil, it's this black, elliptical pill that isn't like any other pill she's ever seen before. And at night he has nightmares, she knows, because she heard him yelling in his sleep.

"Talk to Cohavi," he yelled, "talk to Cohavi." When she asked him about it, he said everything was fine and he doesn't know any Cohavi.

But she knows that he does. Igal Cohavi. His phone number is in Avner's BlackBerry. And of all the numbers listed there, his was the only one she didn't call. She thought he might put a damper on the atmosphere.

"I don't know what's going to happen," Pnina says. "I'm scared."

Mustache nods and says that all four of them should go to Avner's office to see if he's okay.

Eyebrows says that they're all getting a little carried away here and the first thing Pnina should do is call him again. Their phone conversation got cut off; things like that happen all the time. Something might be wrong with Avner, but something might be wrong with the phone company too, and they should check it out before they schlep all the way to Herzliya.

With shaking hands, Pnina punches in Avner's office number. She puts the phone on speaker. Band-Aid thinks that's strange. What if Avner picks up and tells her something intimate or insulting; that could be awkward.

But there's no answer on the other end. Eyebrows says she should try Avner's cell, so Pnina tries. A recorded announcement tells her she's reached Avner Katzman and anyone who needs him urgently should call his secretary or text him because he doesn't listen to messages.

Mustache doesn't know Avner, but just from his diction he can tell he wouldn't like him. There's something haughty about his voice, the voice of someone who thinks everything is coming to him, a kind of noblesse oblige without the oblige.

A lot of the clientele at Mustache's Ra'anana branch were like that, the kind of people who were offended every time the bank charged them a fee. The way they saw it, just agreeing to open an account in Mustache's branch was already a huge gift they'd given to the bank, and how rude, not to mention ungrateful, of the bank to still charge them for a new checkbook or expect them to pay interest on overdrawn funds after they'd made such a lovely gesture.

Eyebrows asks Pnina to text Avner, but Mustache interrupts him, saying they have no more time to waste and they should all drive to his office now. Band-Aid agrees quickly; this whole business seems like an adventure to him.

The truth is that he's not worried about Avner killing himself, because his life insurance policy doesn't cover suicide, but now, even if Band-Aid doesn't get home till four in the morning, he can tell his wife it had to do with work.

They all decide to ride in Mustache's car, a new Honda Civic. In the elevator, Eyebrows still tries to convince them to split up—he and Band-Aid would take his car—but Mustache firmly vetoes the idea.

Band-Aid and Eyebrows sit in the back with their safety belts buckled like two kids on a Saturday family trip. The only thing missing is for Eyebrows to complain to Mustache, "Daddy, Band-Aid's teasing me," or to ask him to stop at a gas station because he has to pee-pee.

Eyebrows, he's capable of stuff like that, a real baby. If there was a war on now, Mustache thinks, and lots of people say there is, Eyebrows is the last person he'd want watching his back. Avner is a pain in the ass, that much is clear already, but still, your patient disappears, his wife is an emotional wreck, and all you can think about is bruschetta and getting home early?

Eyebrows is texting in the back, probably to his wife, probably something sarcastic. Band-Aid is trying to sneak a look at the message, but the angle is wrong. A minute later, when Eyebrows receives an answer, he can read it, and it says, "I'm waiting for you in bed wearing only socks."

That makes Band-Aid jealous. He has never gotten a sexy text message. The last time his wife wanted to say anything sexy to him was before texting was invented, and he doesn't let all those women he fucks on the side text him or leave voice mail. He once read in a newspaper that even if you erase messages, the cell phone company still has copies and they can blackmail you or just screw up your life.

There's heavy traffic all the way to Herzliya. Everyone who works in Tel Aviv is on his way home now. Traffic in the other direction is actually light.

Eyebrows can picture Avner driving home now after a completely ordinary day's work. In that phone conversation, he'd probably wanted to tell Pnina that he loved her, that he's sorry he's been a little stressed-out these last few days, and also for lying about the black pills. They're for hemorrhoids, and he was too embarrassed to tell her, so he tried to sell her a story about headaches.

And when he gets home he'll see some pissed-off people in a caterer's truck fighting over a parking spot with one of the neighbors and he'll think some Buddhist thought like how many of our fights in life are about trivialities, then he'll skip over to the elevator, and when he reaches his floor and opens the door, he'll find a completely empty apartment and a half-empty bottle of cognac.

Pnina won't be there and that'll really hurt. After all, today's his birthday. He doesn't need gifts or parties from her, they're past the age for that kind of crap, but is it too much to ask your life partner to be with you, just be with you on your lousy birthday? And, Eyebrows thinks, at the very same time, Pnina is in a traffic jam on the way to Herzliya. What a joke.

But Avner isn't driving to his apartment in Ramat Aviv now. And he isn't in his office in Herzliya either.

When the four of them finally get there, there's no one in the office, but the security guard at the entrance says he saw Avner leave less than an hour ago. He says Avner had a gun. He knows that because Avner asked him to help cock it. Not that Avner didn't know how to do that, he did, but something was stuck and he wanted the security guard to help him get it unstuck.

Except that the security guard wasn't exactly the right person for the job; he was just an old Kazakh who had grown vegetables in some remote village his whole life, not Rambo. When he came to Israel he asked to work as a farmer, but the people in the agency said no, only Thais and Arabs work in farming today, and what he can do from now till he dies is retire or be a security guard.

He tells Mustache that when he couldn't help with the gun, Avner got angry at him and even started cursing.

"It's not nice," the security guard says. "It's not nice to curse a man my age. And for what? I did something wrong?"

Mustache nods. He knows that if he wants to, he can calm down the security guard too, but he doesn't have the energy anymore. And that talk about the gun bothers him. All the way here he was thinking Pnina might be exaggerating with all that worrying of hers, but now he sees she's really right.

"If he asked me about agriculture, I could help him with everything," the guard says to Band-Aid. "I like to help. But about guns, I don't know. So that is a reason to curse?"

On the way back to the car, Pnina is crying. Eyebrows says that this whole business is out of their hands now, they have to call the police.

Band-Aid butts in, claiming that the police won't do a thing. If you don't have connections, it takes at least a day before they start moving their asses. Not that Band-Aid has a better plan than going to the police, but Eyebrows has been getting on his nerves for a while now and the last thing he wants is to agree with him about anything.

Mustache strokes Pnina's hair. He doesn't have a plan either; he can't think at all while she's crying. Her tears flood his brain, drowning all thoughts before they can be completed. And the fact that Band-Aid and Eyebrows are arguing next to him—that doesn't exactly help his concentration either.

"You two take a taxi. You can't help here anymore," he tells them.

"What about you and Pnina?" Band-Aid asks. He really doesn't want to go, or pay for a cab, or drive all the way to Ramat Aviv with Eyebrows.

Mustache shrugs. He has no answer for that.

"He's right," Eyebrows says, knowing that this is his chance to take off, and besides, Mustache is really right, the fact that there are four of them doesn't help anything. Mustache can drive to the police station with Pnina alone, he doesn't need them to come along and hold his hand.

Band-Aid isn't happy with the whole idea; now that there's a gun and some action, going home would be a real bummer. If he stays he can change something, maybe save that Avner; and even if he doesn't and he just finds his body with Mustache and Pnina, that would be an experience he'd probably remember for the rest of his life. Maybe not the greatest experience, but still, an experience.

He hasn't had too many of those these last few years. There was the blast wave of that missile landing near their vacation *tzimmer* in the north, shattering the window, and a basketball game he went to once with a friend and the TV cameras caught him yawning. Maybe also when his son was born. Even though he wasn't really there for it. His wife made him leave the delivery room a few minutes before because she was angry at him for answering a call from someone at work.

In short, Band-Aid isn't hot on leaving, but he knows that if Mustache and Eyebrows are against him, he can't insist on staying without seeming like an asshole. The only way to save the situation now is to come up with an idea. A killer idea that'll lead to a plan and put him right in the center of things as the originator, someone useful, someone worth having around.

"We have to talk to Igal Cohavi," he says, partly to Mustache, partly to Pnina, who's done crying now and is just panting. "Pnina said she has his number from Avner's BlackBerry. And if he had a dream about him that made him yell, Avner must really have him on his mind. Who knows, that whole story with the gun makes it look like he's going to commit suicide, but what if he's planning to kill that Cohavi instead? We should call and warn him, find out."

As soon as Band-Aid says *commit suicide*, Pnina starts crying again, and when he says *kill*, she faints dead away.

Luckily, Mustache manages to catch her a second before her face hits the sidewalk.

Band-Aid runs over to Mustache to help, but the look on Mustache's face makes it clear that that's not a good idea.

Eyebrows says it's nothing, just the pressure. Someone should get her a glass of water, sit her down on a bench, and she'll be on her feet in no time.

"Get out of here, both of you," Mustache yells, "get out of here now!"

Later, in the taxi, Band-Aid will tell Eyebrows that Mustache went too far; who is he to open a mouth like that to them? These days, if an officer talks to his soldiers like that, he gets a formal complaint lodged against him, so who the hell is Mustache to yell that way at two people he barely knows and who are only trying to help?

That's what he'll say later, in the taxi. But now, outside the office building in Herzliya Pituach, Band-Aid doesn't say anything, and he and Eyebrows walk away, leaving Mustache and Pnina alone.

Mustache carries her to the car and puts her in the passenger seat gently, as if she were a fragile object. Pnina comes to even before they reach the car and mumbles something, her eyes half-closed, but only after he puts her down does he start to listen.

"I'm thirsty," she says.

"I know," Mustache says. "I don't have any water in the car, I'm sorry. We can drive somewhere to buy a bottle. On the way here, really close by, I saw a branch of Aroma."

"You think he's dead already?" she asks.

"Who?" Mustache asks.

He knows who she means but pretends not to—that's a trick meant to make her fear seem unfounded. She looks at him but doesn't say "Avner" like he thought she would. All she does is look at him.

"I'm sure he's fine," Mustache says. His voice sounds convincing. It's the voice that got him the Ra'anana branch and now the one in Ramat Aviv.

"I'm scared," Pnina says, just as he'd imagined her saying it the first time he saw her that evening. She's so beautiful when she says it.

Mustache leans forward and kisses her dry lips. Her lips move away from his. He doesn't see anything, doesn't even notice her hand move, but his cheek feels the slap.

When Eyebrows gets home, his wife is already asleep. He doesn't feel the slightest bit tired. His body is exploding with adrenaline. Eyebrows's mind knows that all the fainting and waiting and weird arguments tonight were all about nothing, but his body is stupid enough to take it seriously. Instead of getting into bed, he sits down in front of the computer and checks his e-mail.

The only message he has is from some jerk who went to elementary school with him and found his e-mail address through an Internet site.

That's what's so frustrating about all that technology,

Eyebrows thinks. The ones who invented the Internet were geniuses and probably believed they were advancing humanity, but in the end, instead of people using all that ingenuity to do research and gain knowledge, they use it to harass some poor guy who sat next to them in the fourth grade.

What exactly is he supposed to write back to that Yiftach Rozales? You remember how we drew a line right down the middle of the desk? How you used to elbow me in the ribs when I crossed it?

Eyebrows tries to imagine what Yiftach Rozales's life is like if all he has to do in his free time is search for some kid he never really liked who was in his class thirty years ago.

After a few minutes of feeling superior to Rozales, Eyebrows starts thinking about himself. And exactly what is he doing with his life? Bending over smelly mouths, drilling and filling cavities in rotten teeth.

"A highly respected profession," that's what his mother always says when she talks about dentistry.

What's to respect? What actually is the difference between being a dentist and being a plumber? They both work in smelly holes, drilling and filling openings to make a living. Both earn decent money. And it's highly probable that neither one really enjoys his profession.

Except that Eyebrows's work is "highly respected," and to gain that respect, Eyebrows had to leave the country for five years to study in Romania while the plumber probably had to invest a little less time.

Today was really the worst, operating on the gums of that old man who never stopped wailing and bleeding, practically choking on the suction. And Eyebrows, who kept trying to calm him down, couldn't stop thinking that it was all for nothing. That it would take that old man at least a year of suffering to get used to the implants and probably two days before or after that he'll die of a heart attack or cancer or a stroke or whatever it is people his age die of.

There should be an age limit for patients, he thinks as he takes off his shoes. You just have to say to them, "You lived long enough. From now on, think of what's left as a bonus, a gift without an exchange slip. It hurts? Stay in bed. It still hurts? Wait: Either you'll die or it'll pass."

That age, Eyebrows thinks to himself as he brushes his teeth, is on its way to me, galloping like a wild horse spraying foam from its nostrils. Soon it'll be me lying in that bed, not getting up. And something about that thought comforts him.

The last time, the only other time that Pnina ever slapped someone, it was Avner. That was seventeen years ago. He wasn't rich yet, or bitter or balding, but he already exuded that confidence that everything was his. It was their first date and they went to a restaurant.

Avner was nasty to the waiter and made him take back his food, which wasn't fantastic, but decent enough. She couldn't figure out what she was doing at the same table with that arrogant guy.

Her roommate had fixed them up. She'd told Pnina that Avner was brilliant and she'd told Avner that Pnina was charming, which was actually her way of saying that she was pretty without feeling like a chauvinist.

Avner spent the whole evening talking to her about stocks and derivatives and institutional investors and didn't let her get a word in edgewise. After dinner he drove her to her apartment in his battered white Autobianchi. He stopped in front of her building, turned off the engine, and suggested going up with her.

She said she didn't think that was a good idea. He reminded her that he knew her roommate and that he just wanted to go upstairs for a minute to say hello to her. Hello and thanks for introducing them.

Pnina smiled politely and said that her roommate would be back late because she was working the night shift. She promised to give her his regards and pass on his thanks and already had the door open to get out, but Avner closed it and kissed her.

There was no hesitation, no wondering how she felt there on the other side of the kiss. It was just a kiss on the mouth, but it felt like rape.

Pnina slapped him and got out of the car. Avner didn't try to follow or call her. From the apartment balcony, she could see his Autobianchi standing there, not moving. For maybe an hour. It was still there when Pnina went to sleep.

In the morning, a delivery guy woke her with a huge and slightly tasteless bouquet of flowers. There was only one word written on the card. *Sorry.*

"I'm sorry," Mustache says, "I didn't mean it."

And Pnina could have been tough on him, could have asked him what exactly did he mean, kissing her? Taking advantage of her weakness? Driving all the way to Herzliya with her in a car that smelled of coconut air deodorizer mixed with sweat? But she doesn't say anything, she doesn't have the strength. She just wants Mustache to take her home.

"Maybe we should go to the police," Mustache says, "just to be on the safe side."

But Pnina says no. Avner will come home in the end, she

just knows it, he's not the kind to commit suicide or shoot someone. After Band-Aid said that, it scared her at first, but now when she tries to picture Avner sticking the gun in his mouth or pressing it against his temple—it's just not him. When she looks at her hands she can see they are shaking, but her mind has already decided that Avner is all right.

Mustache doesn't argue, he just drives Pnina home.

The catering truck is parked outside with two wheels on the sidewalk, still blocking the street. Poor guys, they've been waiting there the whole time. Mustache says he'll get out and talk to them. He wants to help her with something, to make up for what happened. But she doesn't let him. Not to punish him; she just doesn't have the energy.

After Pnina gets out of the car, he calls after her. The rage she felt earlier is gone now. She's not angry at him anymore, really. He actually seems like a nice person. And that kiss—maybe his timing was a little off, but she sensed how much he wanted her from the moment he arrived, and for most of the evening it made her feel good.

Mustache gives her the gift for Avner and his business card, explaining that his cell number is on the card too and she can call him no matter how late. She nods.

She won't call him, not today.

Band-Aid finds a parking spot right outside his building. But instead of going up to the second floor, putting his key in the lock, taking off his clothes in the dark hallway, and creeping quietly to his side of the bed, he starts to walk. At first, he has no idea where he's headed: Shtand Street, King Solomon, King George, then Dizengoff Street. Only on Dizengoff does he realize that he wants to go to the sea.

He keeps walking till he reaches the promenade, and

from there he goes down to the beach. He takes off his shoes and socks and just stands there, scooping up the sand with his toes. Behind him he can hear the noise of traffic, and trance music probably coming from an all-night liquor store. In front of him, he hears the sound of the waves crashing against the breakwater not far from there.

"Excuse me," a young guy with an army buzz cut says, appearing out of nowhere, "you live here?"

Band-Aid nods.

"Great," Buzz Cut says, "so maybe you know where to go for some fun?"

Band-Aid can ask him what kind of fun he means: Alcohol? Girls? A mysterious blast of warmth flooding your chest? What's the point, he doesn't know where to find any of those things, so he just shakes his head.

But Buzz Cut persists. "You said you live here, right?"

Band-Aid doesn't answer, just looks to the distant point where the black of the sea meets the black of the sky.

I wonder what happened to that Avner, he thinks. I hope that in the end, it all worked out.

WHAT ANIMAL ARE YOU?

The sentences I'm writing now are for the benefit of the German Public Television viewers. A reporter who came to my home today asked me to write something on the computer because it always makes for great visuals: an author writing. It's a cliché, she realizes that, but clichés are nothing but an unsexy version of the truth, and her role, as a reporter, is to turn that truth into something sexy, to break the cliché with lighting and unusual angles. And the light in my house falls perfectly, without her having to turn on even a single spot, so all that's left is for me to write.

At first, I just made believe I was writing, but she said it wouldn't work. People would be able to tell right away that I was just pretending. "Write something for real," she demanded, and then, to be sure: "A story, not just a bunch of words. Write naturally, the way you always do." I told her it wasn't natural for me to be writing while I was having my picture taken for German Public Television, but she insisted. "So use it," she said. "Write a story about just that—about how unnatural it seems and how the unnaturalness suddenly produces something real, filled with passion. Something that permeates you, from your brain to your loins. Or the other way around. I don't know how it works with you, what part of your body gets the creative juices flowing. Each person is different." She told me how she'd once interviewed a Belgian author who, every time he wrote, had an erection. Something about the writing "stiffened his organ"—that's the expression she used. It was probably a literal translation from German, and it sounded very strange in English.

"Write," she insisted again. "Great. I love your terrible posture when you write, the cramped neck. It's just wonderful. Keep writing. Excellent. That's it. Naturally. Don't mind me. Forget I'm here."

So I go on writing, not minding her, forgetting she's there, and I'm natural. As natural as I can be. I have a score to settle with the viewers of German Public Television but this isn't the time to settle it. This is the time to write. To write things that will appeal, because when you write crap, she's already reminded me, it comes out terrible on camera.

My son returns from kindergarten. He runs up to me and hugs me. Whenever there's a television crew in the house, he hugs me. When he was younger, the reporters had to ask him to do it, but by now, he's a pro: runs up to me, doesn't look at the camera, gives me a hug, and says, "I love you, Daddy." He isn't four yet, but he already understands how things work, this adorable son of mine.

My wife isn't as good, the German television reporter says. She doesn't flow. Keeps fiddling with her hair, stealing glances at the camera. But that isn't really a problem. You can always edit her out later. That's what's so nice about television. In real life it isn't like that. In real life you can't edit her out, undo her. Only God can do that, or a bus, if it runs her over. Or a terrible disease. Our upstairs neighbor is a widower. An incurable disease took his wife from him. Not cancer, something else. Something that starts in the guts and ends badly. For six months she was shitting blood. At least, that's what he told me. Six months before God Almighty edited her out. Ever since she died, all kinds of women keep visiting our building, wearing high heels and cheap perfume. They arrive at unlikely hours, sometimes as early as noon. He's retired, our upstairs neighbor, and his time is his own. And those women—according to my wife, at least—they're whores. When she says *whores* it comes out natural, like she was saying *turnip*. But when she's being filmed, it doesn't. Nobody's perfect.

My son loves the whores who visit our upstairs neighbor. "What animal are you?" he asks them when he bumps into them on the stairs. "Today I'm a mouse, a quick and slippery mouse." And they get it right away, and throw out the name of an animal: an elephant, a bear, a butterfly. Each whore and her animal. It's strange, because with other people, when he asks them about the animals, they simply don't catch on. But the whores just go along with it.

Which gets me thinking that the next time a television crew arrives I'll bring one of them instead of my wife, and that way it'll be more natural. They look great. Cheap, but great. And my son gets along better with them too. When he asks my wife what animal she is, she always insists: I'm not an animal, sweetie, I'm a person. I'm your mommy." And then he always starts to cry.

Why can't she just go with the flow, my wife? Why is it so easy for her to call women with cheap perfume "whores" but when it comes to telling a little boy "I'm a giraffe" it's more than she can handle? It really gets on my nerves. Makes me want to hit someone. Not her. Her I love. But someone. To take out my frustrations on someone who has it coming. Right-wingers can take it out on Arabs. Racists on blacks. But those of us who belong to the liberal left are trapped. We've boxed ourselves in. We have nobody to take it out on. "Don't call them whores," I rail at my wife. "You don't know for a fact that they're whores, do you? You've never seen anyone pay them or anything, so don't call them that, okay? How would you feel if someone called you a whore?"

"Great," the German reporter says. "I love it. The crease in your forehead. The frenzied keystrokes. Now all we need are an intercut with translations of your books in different languages, so our viewers can tell how successful you are—and that hug from your son one more time. The first time he ran up to you so quickly that Jörg, our cameraman, didn't have a chance to change the focus." My wife wants to know if the German reporter needs her to hug me again too, and in my heart I pray she'll say yes. I'd really love my wife to hug me again, her smooth arms tightening around me, as if there's nothing else in the world but us. "No need," the German says in an icy voice. "We've got that already." "What animal are you?" my son asks the German, and I quickly translate into English. "I'm not an animal," she laughs, running her long fingernails through his hair. "I'm a monster. A monster that came from across the ocean to eat pretty little children like you." "She says she's a songbird," I translate to my son with impeccable naturalness. "She says she's a red-feathered songbird, who flew here from a faraway land."

TRANSLATION ACKNOWLEDGMENTS

"Bad Karma," "Big Blue Bus," "Black and Blue," "Guava," "Healthy Start," "Hemorrhoid," "Lieland," "Mourners' Meal," "Mystique," "Parallel Universes," "The Polite Little Boy," "Suddenly, a Knock on the Door," "Unzipping," and "What Animal Are You?" were translated by Miriam Shlesinger.

"Bitch," "Cheesus Christ," "Creative Writing," "A Good One," "Grab the Cuckoo by the Tail," "Joseph," "Not Completely Alone," "Pick a Color," "September All Year Long," "Shut," "Simyon," "Snot," "Surprise Party," and "What Do We Have in Our Pockets?" were translated by Sondra Silverston.

"Ari," "One Step Beyond," "Pudding," "The Story, Victorious," "Teamwork," "Upgrade," and "What, of This Goldfish, Would You Wish?" were translated by Nathan Englander.